Books by Kara Jorges

California Dream
Cartoon Hero
Act of Love
All Work, No Play
Heart on Ice
Nobody But You

The Nights Trilogy

Nights at the Cuzco
Nights in Captivity
Nights on the Run

California Dream

A Novel By

Kara Jorges

California Dream

© 1990, 2010 by Kara Jorges

All rights reserved. Except for use in any review, the reproduction or utilization of this work in whole or in part in any form by any electronic, mechanical, or other means, now known or hereafter invented, including xerography, photocopying, and recording, or in any information storage or retrieval system, is forbidden without the written permission of the author.

This is a work of fiction. Names, characters, places, and incidents are either the product of the author's imagination or used fictitiously. Any resemblance to actual persons, living or dead, business establishments, events, or locales is entirely coincidental.

California Dream

CHAPTER ONE

Roddy O'Neill was a bad boy, and women loved him for it. For the past ten years, he had wooed them with his voice of liquid gravel, singing songs of lust and love, passion and pain. Women of all ages, shapes, and sizes had fallen prey to the words they were sure he had written just for them. Roddy never let them know that all their faces had begun to blur, and that there had been enough of them to create a directory the size of New York City's phone book.

At twenty-nine, Roddy wasn't slowing down. His tastes had become more particular over the years as his fame grew, but that didn't seem to reduce the constant pace of the revolving door into his bedroom. Roddy was a rock star, and women came with the territory.

What had always amused him about his appeal with the opposite sex were his looks. He wasn't classically handsome, and in his opinion, not really all that good looking. His dirty-blond hair was long and often unkempt, he did not have the soulful eyes of a poet, and did not possess perfectly-straight, gleaming-white teeth. He filled out a pair of leather pants rather nicely, though, and while not huge and buff, he worked out to keep the rest of his body in shape.

Roddy knew it was all about his renegade attitude and rock and roll wardrobe. What woman with a pulse didn't like a rock star in leather pants? He wore his shirts unbuttoned to the waist, a bandanna usually held his hair back from his face, and he had a penchant for real snakeskin boots. The look had certainly worked for him, even if he didn't have a pretty boy face. He knew his music was a big part of what drew the women, but it was really more about his image. Any musician, successful rock star or not, could get girls. It didn't matter if his music was any good or not.

Supposing his birthday was making him introspective, Roddy lay back with his feet up and let his mind wander back to the early days while he drifted off to sleep on the tour bus. Success was a given these days, but it hadn't always been that way. There had been the usual struggles, and he hadn't been able to believe it at first when his records soared high on the charts and the money started pouring in. Of course, he had reacted in typical rock star fashion, and allowed himself to fall into a pit of alcohol and drug abuse that very nearly destroyed his career.

That was over now. He was back on top with a new number-one song and life couldn't be better.

It didn't bother him that he had to go onstage in Minneapolis on his twenty-ninth birthday. Screaming fans were a great way to celebrate, and he could take his pick of which one he wanted for his present. He

CALIFORNIA DREAM

was well past the point of picking the ones that were too young, of course, and some nights he refused them all. He was young, single, and healthy, though, so that didn't happen very often.

Satisfied with life in general, Roddy drifted off to sleep. There would be plenty of time to think about his backstage pickings after the show. They were all the same anyway.

ଔ

"Roddy O'Neill tickets! No way!" Lee Miller vaulted off her chair and flew into her best friend's embrace.

Her best friend Debbie smiled broadly. "Jim has connections. He hates Roddy, so I convinced him to let us take the tickets."

"Remind me to tell Jim how much I love him!" Lee said, squealing and giving Debbie another hug.

At five minutes before quitting time on Friday afternoon, it was easy for Lee and Debbie to forget themselves and proper library etiquette. A frown from their boss, Mr. Eggers, quieted them and sent them penitently back to their desks.

"What should I wear?" Lee whispered.

"Leather," Debbie said with a shrug.

At the stroke of five, Lee and Debbie dashed out the door, ignoring the disapproving glare from Mr. Eggers.

"The concert's at eight, so I'll pick you up at six-thirty," Debbie told Lee before they parted ways.

"I'll be waiting on my front steps!"

Lee vowed she would wait all night and day in freezing rain if it meant she would get Roddy O'Neill tickets out of the experience.

Thinking about Debbie's fashion advice, Lee threw open her closet doors and glared at the contents inside. She really didn't own a lot of leather, and what she had wasn't very tough-looking. She owned nothing with wicked studs, but she was in possession of a lime-green biker jacket with huge buckles and lots of zippers. Though the color would have been laughed out of any local biker bar, it suited Lee and the style seemed just right for the concert that night.

Lee paired the jacket with tight, faded jeans that had a tear in the left knee and a plain white tee-shirt. Her long, streaky-blonde hair was allowed to tumble in disarray down her back, as it would never be seen in the library. For shoes, she selected a pair of high-top sneakers with laces that matched her jacket.

She smiled jauntily at her image in the mirror. Complete with huge gold hoop earrings that peeped through her hair from time to time, she could pass for any age from seventeen to twenty-seven. The ambiguity seemed perfect for a Roddy O'Neill concert. For some reason, she craved an air of mystery that night.

Debbie's remarks convinced Lee that she had chosen the right outfit, though hers wasn't quite as racy as Debbie's black leather mini-dress and matching boots.

Target Center, the concert venue, was packed to the gills. It only added to Lee's excitement. She and Debbie had good seats, up front and center. Lee barely heard the opening act in her anticipation of finally being able to see Roddy O'Neill perform live, and when they finished and the fans started screaming, "Roddy! Roddy!" she added her voice to the melee.

Roddy O'Neill was Lee's favorite rock star, and she had the same kind of crush on him that any young woman had on her favorite celebrity. She found her attraction rising a notch from the moment Roddy strutted out on stage, and by halfway through his first number, she was thoroughly hooked. His thrusting, prancing gyrations got her imagination going, and it just didn't matter that every woman in the place probably felt the same way. It was part of his unique charisma.

Debbie had a special surprise for Lee that night, but Lee had to wait until Roddy and his band ran off stage after their last encore before it was revealed.

"Oh, there's one more thing," Debbie said almost casually while the girls prepared to leave.

When Lee turned to give her a quizzical look, Debbie flashed a pair of backstage passes. Lee's mouth dropped open and her eyes went wide.

"Ohmygod!" she screamed, her feet leaving the floor.

Debbie grinned. "Come on! Quit gawking and let's go to the party!"

Both young women garnered a lot of stares as they made their way through backstage security. They were two young beauties wearing eye-catching outfits, hoping to meet with stars. Backstage security had seen just about everything, but they still weren't above appreciating attractive women, particularly since they often got their pick of Roddy O'Neill's leavings.

The party room was a zoo by the time Debbie and Lee got there. Camera flashes went off almost constantly, and champagne corks seemed to pop every few seconds. There were platters of food laid out on a long table that went mostly ignored. Deep in the center of the crowd, Roddy's band was surrounded by avid young fans, but the star himself was nowhere in sight.

☙

His fans didn't know it, but Roddy hated backstage parties. Even though they yielded his evening's entertainment, he was tired of the cameras, the constant questions, and even the endless succession of women with adulation in their eyes. The action backstage was vital to his career, though. He had to keep up a constant appearance of affability if he didn't want to see nasty stories about himself in the gossip rags. Since it was his birthday, though, he decided his appearance that night would be very brief.

He entered the room between Bart and Lester, his two burly bodyguards. A barrage of flashes immediately erupted in his face, and he gritted his teeth and smiled through it. It seemed the tabloids loved nothing more than to print unflattering pictures. If he didn't smile, his face would appear on them accompanied by false stories of his ugly temper tantrums. Bart snatched him a glass of champagne and he started his perfunctory rounds of the room.

Eddie Brandon was Roddy's lead guitarist. Eddie was handsome, in a bad boy kind of way, and always managed to find attractive women. He had the requisite pair of young girls waiting when he beckoned Roddy.

At least the girls looked young, Roddy mused. Something in the blonde's eyes gave her away. Her demeanor was the same as any other fan's, but her gaze was deep and promising. If he wasn't mistaken, she looked a little hungry...for him. Her stare was rather predatory, actually, and not at all the adoration he was used to. Roddy also took note that it was just for him; the blonde barely even glanced at Eddie.

Roddy felt his body responding to her. Even with all his conquests, he had never seen anything quite like the way she looked at him. The woman's eyes offered him a challenge that sent a slight shiver up his spine. He got the feeling *he* would be a notch on *her* belt. Her eyes told him she would take more than she gave, and she would expect satisfaction.

Roddy suddenly forgot about his earlier plans. He no longer felt like skipping out early and going back to his room to write music until he got tired enough to fall asleep. Just then, the blonde seemed like a most intriguing option.

As he stood there gazing at her and her friend, he found his interest in her increasing. He wasn't quite sure how, but she made him feel like she had chosen him out of a crowd instead of the other way around. He was used to being in complete control when it came to women, but he had the feeling he was out of his element that night.

Naturally, the blonde presented quite an attractive package. She had a lean, shapely body that looked like she spent a lot of time engaged in outdoor sports. He longed to run his fingers through the riot of streaky hair that tumbled down her back. Her face was breathtaking. She had huge green eyes, soft, sensual lips, a straight nose, and an almost belligerent set to her chin.

"Hello," he rasped when he got up close. His voice was hoarse after the show. "I'm Roddy O'Neill."

Her eyes flashed just slightly when she smiled. "I know who you are."

Eddie sidled closer. "And I'm Eddie Brandon, guitar player extraordinaire."

"Hi, Eddie." The blonde gave him a smile, but it was several degrees cooler than the one she bestowed on Roddy.

It made him scowl. Eddie wasn't used to women who ignored him, but Roddy supposed it just wasn't his night.

The blonde turned her eyes back on Roddy. "You must be exhausted," she said. "If I danced around like that for two straight hours, I'd be ready to drop."

"We're tough, we can take it," Eddie answered for him, earning a look that was just shy of cold.

The surprise that quickly passed on Eddie's face said he knew the score. The blonde had eyes only for Roddy.

Roddy's behavior over the past couple of years had confused his band. He still partied and still took his backstage pickings, but he seemed to have largely lost interest in it. He no longer participated in the rock star lifestyle with as much enthusiasm as he once had. It was almost as if he half-heartedly went along with everyone else because it was the thing to do.

That was about to change. A quick glance around revealed no one else of interest in the room. No surprise there. Smiling to himself, he decided to take the blonde up on her unspoken offer.

First, though, he had to get through the social niceties.

The blonde's friend, whom he had quite frankly forgotten, seemed willing to soothe Eddie's battered ego. She smiled up at him and introduced herself as Debbie, then gushed on and on about how much she loved the way he played the guitar. Eddie, of course, ate it up.

As if they had known each other for years, Roddy and the blonde caught each other's gaze and rolled their eyes. Debbie and Eddie were oblivious to the electricity between them, more interested in the chemistry they might find in each other, so Roddy smiled and took his chance.

"Wanna get out of here?" he asked.

Eddie and Debbie suddenly went silent, but Roddy and the blonde took no notice. The only thing they noticed at the moment was each other.

"I'd love to," she said with a grin.

༄

Lee was proud of herself for casually smiling at Roddy O'Neill like backstage parties were an everyday, boring occurrence for her, too. She was tempted to peek at her feet to see if they were still touching the floor.

A glance at Debbie showed she suddenly got the gist of what was happening, and that her flirtation with Eddie might be serious stakes. Just because Lee was ready to step outside the bounds of her life and do something irresponsible and exciting didn't mean Debbie would. No doubt, Eddie Brandon was just a little too fast for a girl like her.

She tugged at Lee's sleeve. "Can I talk to you for a minute?"

Lee gave Roddy a smile and allowed Debbie to pull her aside.

Debbie's eyes were narrowed with concern. "Are you sure about this? How are you going to get home?"

Lee knew she was being wild and irresponsible, but this was *Roddy O'Neill* and she couldn't make herself care. She squeezed Debbie's hand and her eyes implored her to understand.

"I'll be fine," she assured her friend. "If Roddy doesn't get me home, I can call a cab."

"There's a party at Arnie's. You're going to miss it."

Lee met her friend's gaze for a long moment. "We can compare notes tomorrow."

She stepped back over to Roddy O'Neill and met his questioning look with one of firm decision.

A glance at Eddie revealed he and Debbie did not share the same chemistry. His eyes were already checking out other women in the room, and he almost gratefully sidled away when Roddy took Lee's arm to lead her toward the door.

"You kids have fun!" Eddie tossed over his shoulder while he headed toward a gaggle of women clustered around the drummer.

Lee met Debbie's eyes, and her friend gave her a wink. The night had only just begun.

CHAPTER TWO

"Thirsty?" Roddy asked once they were seated in the back of his limousine. He indicated the well-stocked bar in the back.

"Not really," she told him. Her eyes lazily roved over the interior of the car.

Roddy decided not to waste any more time. He glanced once out the window at the passing city lights, then tossed an arm over her shoulder and leaned in.

"You've got some very sexy lips," he murmured in her ear.

"Thank you," she breathed with a flutter of lashes. "I like yours, too."

"Then maybe they should get to know each other," he said, letting loose with just a little of the desire he already knew might get out of control. His lips descended and softly urged hers to open beneath him.

Her response was a pleasant surprise. He wasn't sure who had their fingers in the other's hair first, but the moment he touched her, the promised passion between them reared up and took over. He found himself swept away by the instant attraction, a feeling that was downright rare for a man with his history. Usually, women were pliant and eager to please. This one seemed to know exactly what she wanted from him, and just how to get it.

"That was a little unexpected," he breathed when they came up for air.

"Mmm," was all she said, gazing at him with her unfathomable, half-lidded green eyes.

She made no move to kiss him again, choosing instead to wait for him to take the lead. She simply inflamed him. She was by turns both aggressive and demure. She let him make all the first moves, but when he did, she responded with intensity.

Roddy couldn't even remember the ride back to his hotel, and had only the barest recollection of their stumbling journey through the lobby. All he could recall was how the desk clerk scowled at the way they had their hands all over each other, and how he gave the man a broad wink when the elevator doors slid shut on the tawdry scene within.

It would be a long time before he was able to forget what happened when they got back to his room. The door had barely shut behind them when they started tearing each other's clothes off. Everything seemed to burst into flames when they came together with such incredible intensity, and afterwards, he was both speechless and breathless from the encounter.

He was disoriented awhile later when he woke up. Usually, there was bright sunlight streaming through his windows when he awakened, but it was dark this time, and he was not alone. The blonde still lay sleeping at his side.

That was different. He usually sent his women away long before he even considered going to sleep. He had a pattern: take them to his room, enjoy them, give them a trinket or some piece of Roddy O'Neill memorabilia, and then shove them out the door. After, he liked to stay up half the night chain smoking with the band members who straggled in at all hours, and he generally went to sleep right around the time the sun was creeping over the horizon.

He scowled at the woman sleeping beside him. What was it about her? The passion he shared with her went so far off the charts, it knocked him out afterwards. He still felt more as if she had used him than the other way around. It didn't matter that he was the world-famous rock star who usually did the using. The blonde beside him obviously lived by her own rules.

He wasn't the slightest bit upset by her lack of awe for him. He wouldn't admit it to the other guys, but he liked the way she acted like they were equals. Somewhere along the line, he had begun to tire of adoring women who threw themselves at him, as if he was something slightly above human and it might rub off on them. Even if he treated them poorly, they came back begging for more.

This woman was different. Belatedly, he realized he still didn't know her name. She also had not told him she loved him or adored him, and had not offered to do whatever he liked. He was sure words like that never passed her luscious lips.

The more he awakened, the more it started to

bother him that she knew who he was, but he had no idea about her. He wasn't really sure why, since he usually didn't care about women's backgrounds or personal lives. As she lay sleeping beside him, though, he began to wonder who she was and what she did for a living. Her clothes told him almost nothing, since everybody wore jeans and tee-shirts. The only clue to her personality was her rather bizarre leather jacket and matching sneakers. They said absolutely nothing about her name or what she did. They only confirmed what he had known since their eyes first met: she was an original.

Inspiration suddenly struck.

Quietly, so as not to disturb her, Roddy climbed out of bed and unearthed his jeans. They weren't so easy to find, as he had flung them across the room once he managed to free himself of their confines, and they were halfway under an endtable. He pulled them on, picked up his guitar and cigarettes, and then settled into a chair.

His fingers seemed to find the chords on their own. He strummed quietly, never considering that the noise might awaken her. In Roddy's world, one got used to sleeping under all sorts of conditions. A softly-strummed acoustic guitar should have been soothing, in his opinion, so just as softly, he began to sing the words that came to mind while he played.

> I think I could love her
> If only she'd tell me her name
> Someday I could love her
> 'Cause she never played my games

> I know if I loved her
> My life wouldn't be the same...

The blonde awakened while he sat in the corner playing his guitar, and he caught her watching him with a smile on her lips. From her serene posture, Roddy guessed she didn't realize the song was about her, or maybe he wasn't singing loud enough for her to catch the lyrics. Still, he set his guitar aside when he noticed she had awakened. Just because she inspired him didn't mean he wanted her to know.

"New song?" she asked as his voice trailed off.

He gave her a smile and ignored the question. "Did I wake you? I'm sorry."

She smiled back. "Don't apologize. I liked it."

Roddy just kept smiling at her.

"I'm not about to complain about a private performance from Roddy O'Neill," she told him while sitting up in the bed.

"What do you do?" he asked out of the blue.

She looked away for a moment. "I'm a clerk in a library."

"You're kidding. Really?"

"Not your vision of a librarian? I don't dress like this for work. I mean, what I was wearing when I was dressed." She suddenly looked a little embarrassed about sitting there naked.

"No, I don't suppose," Roddy agreed. He sat back in his chair and stared a little harder at her. "A librarian, huh? A smart girl."

"Hardly," she scoffed. "I'm a clerk, not a librarian.

CALIFORNIA DREAM

If I was smart, I'd have a much better job."

"Like mine," he said on a laugh. "Only nobody thinks I'm smart."

"I wouldn't go that far."

"Oh? So you came here for my brains?" He raised an eyebrow.

She looked away for a second, then pinned him with her eyes. "I came here for you. I think you're incredibly talented, and a modern poet."

"The critics would disagree."

"Because you scream your poetry over electric guitars?"

He smiled at the serious look on her face. "Yes."

She smiled back. "It's infinitely more fun to listen to it that way than just reading it."

He just stared at her for a few seconds. "I like the way you talk," he said finally. "You sound like, I don't know…"

"A librarian?"

"Yeah." They just stared into each other's eyes for a few more seconds, and then he asked, "Why did you come back here with me? I know it's not the usual you."

She swallowed but did not look away. "Because I wanted you."

The straightforward words froze him for a moment. He wasn't used to such blunt honesty from women.

"You're not like anyone else I've ever met," he told her.

"Seriously?"

He paused, not knowing how to explain it without

insulting her or hurting her feelings. "Sure. I mean, well, you know how it is."

"Not really."

He decided she deserved as much honesty as she gave. "There have been a lot of women, and they're all the same. They love to service a rock star."

"I didn't come here just because you're a rock star," she said evenly, and without pique. Her words were actually rather thoughtful. "I'm sure it helped because I wouldn't have known who you were otherwise, but I came here because you're you. I like *you*. I like what you say in your music, and the way you say it. You've got one hell of a stage presence, and then when we met after the concert, I felt something between us."

"I know what you mean. I felt it, too," he admitted carefully, not wanting to lead her on when he wasn't in a position to make promises. He was leaving in the morning, after all.

She held his gaze with hers as she went on. "If you hadn't invited me back here with you, I wouldn't have chased after you or anything. But I think I would have been disappointed."

Roddy didn't tell her he forgot there were any other women in the room from the moment their eyes met. He also didn't bother explaining how bored he had become with everything lately, until he laid eyes on her. They were things he wasn't ready to digest yet himself, and he certainly couldn't share them with her.

"Will you sing for me again?" she asked tentatively.

She looked so sweet and innocent, lying in his

rumpled bed. At that moment, Roddy would have done just about anything she asked.

He reached for his guitar and raised a brow at her. "What do you want to hear?"

"Something that's not on any of your CDs."

He immediately obliged, slipping into a new song. It was a soft and melodious piece about falling in love, and his gravelly voice rasped through the melody. Her eyes warmed while he sang, and he found himself almost unable to look away, enjoying the connection between them.

"Do you always melt girls' hearts that way?" she asked when he finished and his fingers stilled on the guitar strings.

"You made the request," he told her, slipping into another slow song that had at one time topped the charts.

Recognizing it, her soft voice joined his.

"You've got some nice pipes," he complimented with sincerity when the song was over.

"Not exactly professional grade. I like yours better."

"The critics hate it. They say I'm just a screamer."

"Critics have no talent, and they're probably all old men."

"Do you like working in that library?"

"For now, but not forever. Someday I'll find my niche."

"How old are you?"

"Twenty-three."

"And trying to find your groove." Roddy's voice sounded wistful. "I've been in mine since I was sixteen. All I ever wanted to do was rock and roll."

"You're lucky. I can't think of a single career I'd want to do forever," she said with a rueful look. "I certainly don't have the driving ambition it takes to be an entertainer."

"You've got something."

She scowled and seemed to close up. "Right. You're just saying that. You don't really know anything about me."

"Hardly seems fair, does it? I mean, you know all sorts of things about me."

"Just the stuff they write in magazines. I don't know anything important."

He set the guitar on the floor next to his chair and stood up to stretch. "You know my name. You still haven't told me yours."

"You're right, I haven't."

She simply lay there against the pillows and watched him advance on her, slowly unzipping his jeans along the way. When he reached the bed and sat on the mattress beside her, she made room for him. His mouth unerringly found hers again, and his arms came around her.

This time was different. This time, she gave herself to him, all warm, willing woman. He plundered her expertly, even tenderly, with slow, deliberate movements that lacked none of the intensity of what had come before.

When it was over and she slept beside him again, Roddy realized she still hadn't told him her name. He had come right out and asked her, and she still evaded him. He wasn't sure why she was being secretive, but it intrigued him.

Well, he had his ways.

He rolled out of bed and found her purse under her bright green jacket. He hunkered down, tossed a furtive glance at the blonde in his bed, and unzipped the bag to dump its contents on the floor. Lipstick, a wallet, a checkbook, and assorted female odds and ends tumbled into a pile on the carpet. Roddy scooped up everything but the checkbook and shoved it back inside. He ripped a deposit slip out of the back of the checkbook and smiled when he noted it listed both her address and phone number. Hoping she wouldn't catch him in the act of snooping through her most personal possessions, he stuck the checkbook back in her purse, zipped it up, and stashed it back under her jacket. The deposit slip was folded and shoved into his pocket.

He had barely straightened when a loud knock sounded at the door. Roddy wrapped a towel around his waist before going to answer it.

"Hey, Rod, been sleeping?" Eddie tried to peer past Roddy's shoulder into the room.

Roddy grimaced and moved to block his view. "Not really, no."

"Get rid of her and come on. The party's in my room tonight."

Roddy scowled at the thought of "getting rid" of the blonde. Ordinarily, such a turn of phrase wouldn't have fazed him at all, but he found himself bothered by it that night.

He faked a yawn. "Not tonight, Ed. Just don't feel up to it. We have to be on the road pretty early tomorrow anyway."

Eddie cracked a huge grin and winked. "Sure. No problem, man. Just make sure you get some sleep, huh?"

"Get lost." Roddy gave his best friend a cheerful smile and shut the door after Eddie turned away.

Not until the guitarist had gone did Roddy realize he was bored. The blonde was passed out cold in the middle of his bed, and at the moment he didn't feel like waking her for another round. He was no longer in the mood to play guitar, which would awaken her. Going back to sleep just wasn't going to happen. He still wasn't quite sure he felt like hanging out with the band all night, either. The thought of sitting around, catching a buzz, breathing in smoky air, and watching Eddie romance yet another girl who was totally in awe of them all held no appeal.

Impulsively, the way Roddy did nearly everything, he decided to awaken the blonde. Why not invite her to the party with the band? Eddie brought girls just about everywhere he went and nobody thought a thing of it. That it would be a first for Roddy shouldn't matter a bit.

CHAPTER THREE

"Wake up, sleepy," a voice said softly, shaking her shoulder.

"Go away," Lee mumbled. "It's Saturday. I don't have to work." She burrowed further under the covers.

"I don't want you to work," the voice said with amusement this time. "I want to take you out to play."

Lee's eyes flew open, and it all came rushing back. She smiled up at Roddy O'Neill and stretched just slightly.

"I wasn't expecting you," she murmured.

His eyes narrowed. "Who else would it be?"

She smiled to herself at his possessiveness. The night just kept getting better and better.

He smiled back and started tugging at the sheets. "Come on, get up."

A thought occurred to her, and her smile faded. "Are you kicking me out?"

He scowled for a moment before laughing outright. "No. I want to take you somewhere."

"Oh." She turned pink, remembering he had said he wanted to take her out to play. "I'm sorry. I just thought…"

"Don't worry about it. I have kicked visitors out in the middle of the night," he said with a smile. "But only when they bore me."

"But a library clerk is interesting to you."

"Get your clothes on, librarian," he said on a laugh, tossing her jeans at her.

She sat up, for the moment oblivious to her naked flesh, and dangled her long legs over the side of the bed. She slipped her jeans on, and then stood to regard him with raised brows.

"Have you seen my shirt?" she wondered.

He smiled appreciatively at her. "Did you have one earlier?"

She primly crossed her arms over her chest and reached over to snatch her jacket off the floor and put it on while she hunted down her elusive tee-shirt. She finally found it in a crumpled ball under a chair, but her bra seemed to be a lost cause.

"We can look for the rest of your stuff later," Roddy told her as she pulled her shirt over her head.

She gave herself a cursory glance in the mirror, ran a hand through her hair, and followed him out the door.

She took the time to give Roddy a full perusal while they walked down the hall. He had his hair secured pirate-style under a bandanna, and his thighs bulged under a pair of tight, faded jeans, which were in turn stuffed unceremoniously into a pair of snakeskin boots. He had an unbuttoned shirt thrown carelessly over the ensemble. The whole picture was very sexy, and Lee knew she would have to make an effort not to stare at him with her tongue hanging out all night.

They went just a few doors down the hall, and Roddy was about to knock when the door was suddenly flung open. Eddie Brandon stood on the other side with a cigarette dangling out of his mouth and a shapely blonde under his arm.

He stopped in his tracks when he saw them. "Roddy! You decided to come after all. And look everyone, he brought a girl!"

"Roddy brought a girl?" a disembodied voice came from somewhere in the room.

"Yup, and she's not as ugly as usual. We won't even need to put a bag over her head!"

Roddy turned to Lee. "That was a compliment of sorts," he told her as he ushered her into the room.

To Lee's pleasant surprise, Eddie didn't seem to remember her from earlier in the night. He was a friendly, gracious host who offered her a place to sit and a cold beer, and she tried to relax and act like she partied with rock stars every day.

"I'm Zeke," another long-haired man in jeans told her as he lit a cigarette. "I'm the drummer."

"Hi, Zeke," Lee said, extending her hand. "I know. I'm a big fan of yours."

Zeke indicated the simpering girl at his side. "This is…um…what was your name again, honey?"

"Cindy!" For some reason, being unmemorable threw her into fits of giggles.

Lee decided not to further an acquaintance with Cindy, but the other girl didn't seem to care. Lee wasn't a rock star, and was thus beneath her notice.

Roddy made sure to introduce her to the other members of the band. Lee met David, the bassist, and Mike, who played rhythm guitar. David and Mike also had vacuous dates, and had it not been for Roddy's attentive behavior, she would have felt decidedly out of place.

Lee was amused that the other women there seemed impressed by her career as a library clerk.

"A librarian! Geez!" Cindy exclaimed. "I can't remember the last time I even read a book! Probably when I was in high school."

"Can't have been all that long ago," Lee murmured under her breath, and Roddy heard her and gave her a sideways smile. She turned to him and whispered, "I'm starting to see why you think I'm interesting. I'm not the oldest, but I'm probably the only woman in the room with a diploma."

"That's not very nice," Roddy chastised with an evil grin. "But I think that's why I like you. I'm usually not very nice either. This is why I usually get rid of my pick-ups early in the night."

"The pick-up librarian," Lee mused. "Sounds like a racy novel."

Roddy looked distressed at his careless turn of phrase. "I didn't mean it like that."

"It's okay, Roddy," she assured him. "I know what I am tonight. I don't make a habit of lying to myself."

He still looked uncomfortable at the direction the conversation was taking. "I hope you don't mind if we change the subject," he said with a scowl.

The look she gave him was impish. "Whatever

makes you happy."

He smiled suddenly and leaned over to kiss her. His lips were soft and seductive, and in that moment Lee completely ignored her surroundings. He had a way of making her forget they weren't alone every time he touched her. It would have been easy to simply let go and cling to him, but she brought herself back to earth just in time.

"Need another beer?" Eddie lurched by and interrupted. "There's plenty more in the fridge."

"Yes, I could use another one," Lee said casually, as if she hadn't just been thoroughly kissed by the man of her dreams.

"Me too." Roddy sounded less in control of himself than she was.

○✸

Roddy had the sinking feeling it had been a mistake to bring his blonde to the party that night, though for different reasons than usual. Just looking at her had him coming unglued. Since the moment he laid eyes on her, he stopped following his carefully-crafted pick-up etiquette. He was supposed to use her once, get rid of her, and there was no way he should have introduced her to the band. He certainly shouldn't be standing around in front of them all kissing her like some goggle-eyed teenage kid.

He knew he could blame it all on her. She just didn't play her role the way he was used to seeing it played. She was supposed to idolize him and act like he was the love of her life. Instead, she treated him like he was an average guy. She was also supposed to pull out all the stops to impress him and try to make herself memorable, but the blonde practically came out and told him she knew she was a nameless, faceless nobody, even refusing to part with her name. Though he had it now, that itself was enough to make her unforgettable.

Roddy found it uncomfortable playing his usual game with someone who anticipated his every move and undermined him at every turn. She was friendly, but distant, with the band. Even Eddie didn't faze her. She truly seemed to have eyes only for Roddy. Usually, pick-ups adored the whole band, and were easily interchangeable. It made it easier for everyone if the original set-up wasn't working. Looking around the room, Roddy knew he couldn't muster the slightest bit of interest for any of the other women there.

"Do you do this every night while you're on tour?" His blonde cut into his thoughts with her question.

"Pretty much, unless we're just sick of each other," he told her. "We just got back from a break, though, so we're all getting along tonight. Getting away from each other every now and again helps us work together better."

"It sounds like another family."

"Another?" Eddie scoffed, breaking into their conversation. "Try only. My old man hates me and I know my mom threw a party when I moved out."

"I guess you get the last laugh now," the blonde told him, skipping the phony sympathy Eddie's family remarks usually garnered. "You're a star, and they're not."

CALIFORNIA DREAM

Eddie looked at her strangely. "Sounds like you know a little something about family issues."

She shrugged. "My mother ran off when I was ten, and it's generous to say that my father and I have never been close."

There was some respect in Eddie's gaze after that, but Roddy felt troubled. He was very close to his mother, and couldn't fathom having a family like hers or Eddie's.

"You should trade with me, Roddy," Eddie suggested. "She and I would have lots to talk about."

Roddy very nearly hit him, and Eddie's date uttered an outraged gasp, but the blonde laughed and reached a hand out to stroke Roddy's arm.

"Sometimes I don't feel very conversational," she said with a smile.

Roddy picked up on her cue immediately and took her hand. "I'm a little tired myself. Let's call it a night."

"We leave in the morning," Eddie called out after them.

The blonde turned to give him a saucy grin. "I'll have him home early," she promised.

୧୨

Roddy was surprised at how exhausted he felt when his call jangled him awake the next morning. He was still lying there trying to clear his head when the blonde wordlessly slid out of bed and started collecting her clothes. He stared at her all the while, thinking he might actually miss her when he left. He wasn't all that anxious to say good-bye.

"Can I give you a ride home?" he asked when she

was dressed.

She shook her head. "I'll get a cab."

Roddy sat up and grabbed his jeans off the floor to pull them on. He reached into his pocket and extracted his wallet.

"At least take this." He pulled out a hundred-dollar bill.

She recoiled. "Don't insult me, Roddy."

He frowned deeply. "I don't mean it as an insult. I really like you. I should at least take you out for breakfast or buy you something pretty or something."

He held the bill out again, and this time she took it, but she stuffed it brazenly into his jeans pocket.

"I don't need anything pretty, and when I do I'll buy it for myself. I'm not going to forget you if I don't have a souvenir."

Her words hit home, and Roddy found himself staring speechlessly after her as the door closed softly on her back.

CHAPTER FOUR

The following weekend, while Lee and Debbie sat on her couch watching a movie, the phone rang. She reached over absently to pick it up, and stiffened immediately when she heard a male voice on the other end.

"Hi, Lee." It was Paul West, a guy she had dated a couple of times recently.

Lee liked Paul. He was a sweet guy who worked as a paralegal at a law firm in downtown Minneapolis. He was cute and nice, and she had completely forgotten he even existed from the moment she laid eyes on Roddy O'Neill.

"Oh, hi, Paul." Debbie glanced over when she heard the name and Lee wished she was alone. "How've you been?" She vaguely recalled him telling her something a couple of weeks ago about going to Mexico on vacation and felt a little guilty for not being able to remember the details.

"I'm great! I just got back to town last night and wanted to know if you'd like to go out again," he said with warmth.

Lee's reaction surprised her. She had thought after her night out of time with Roddy O'Neill that she would file the memory away and get back to real life, but now that it had come calling, she was no longer interested. While two weeks ago Paul hadn't exactly made her heart race, she still liked him enough to go out on a couple of dates. Now, the thought made her squirm.

"I'm sorry, Paul," she said with contrition in her tone. "I can't."

"Oh." Disappointment came through loud and clear.

"I'm sorry," she repeated. "I—I met someone else."

At this, Debbie looked at her sharply, but Lee strove to ignore her friend. After Paul mumbled something to end their conversation, Lee hung up and tried to turn her attention back to the TV, but Debbie would have none of it.

"Who is it?" she demanded the second Lee set the phone aside.

"Who is who?"

Debbie sighed. "The other guy you met. The reason you're dumping Paul."

Lee sighed and looked at a blank spot on the wall. Debbie was going to laugh at her, but she couldn't lie to her best friend.

"Roddy O'Neill," she said at last.

"I knew it!" Debbie looked thrilled. "I knew there was something special between you two."

"Yeah, sex," Lee said far less casually than she intended.

Debbie made a noise. "More than that! I could feel it from the second you met."

Lee attempted to brush it off. "You're imagining things. We were attracted to each other and I slept with him, but he's a rock star, Debbie. He does stuff like that every night. I knew what it was all about. I didn't even tell him my name."

Debbie just stared at Lee, obviously wondering what had gotten into her. It wasn't surprising that Lee had spent the night with Roddy O'Neill after the way they took off together. She was just no doubt shocked over Lee's casual attitude about it. Lee supposed her friend thought she should be planning their next date or something, but she knew the real score.

"You haven't told me very many of the details," Debbie said gently. "And I could tell you weren't really ready to talk about it, so I didn't pry."

Lee gave her a long and level look. She was sure Debbie was dying to ask a thousand questions about Roddy O'Neill, and for that reason she had deliberately blown her off for the last few days, except to leave a quick voicemail to say she was all right. Lee was glad Debbie knew her well enough not to press for details she wasn't ready to talk about yet, but also knew Debbie's patience wouldn't last forever. Debbie was her best friend, and if for no other reason, she owed her an explanation.

"There really isn't much to tell," Lee said simply. "He took me to a party in Eddie's room some time in the night. The rest of the band seemed really nice. Mostly, I just hung out with Roddy."

"And?" Debbie's face was expectant.

Lee looked away. "And I'll never forget it. I'm

sorry I deserted you backstage."

Debbie shrugged. "No biggie. I would have done the same thing if I was in your shoes."

Lee smiled, fairly certain Debbie was lying. "That's nice of you to say."

"So? What's next?"

Lee's smile faded. "Nothing. He goes back to his life and I go back to mine. End of story."

Lee just wished it really was that simple, but she already knew Roddy O'Neill would not be easy to forget.

ଔ

Somebody remembered Lee the following Monday. As she and Debbie dragged themselves back to the Research & Cataloging Department after lunch, they were immediately set upon by Mr. Eggers.

"I'll have you know that a number of library patrons have allergies, Miss Miller," was his greeting. His face was tight and he seemed to bite each word as he spit it out.

"I'm not wearing any perfume today," Lee told the little, balding man in the most pleasant tone she could muster.

Mr. Eggers puffed up like a rooster. "I'm not talking about *perfume*," he huffed, dragging out the word as if perfume was an evil substance responsible for the world's decay. "I'm talking about those."

His bony hand shot out to point accusingly at her desk. It was done with such ferocity, Lee half expected lightning to spark from his fingertips.

Nothing could have prepared her for the sight on her desk, though.

"That's got to be the biggest bouquet of red roses I've ever seen!" Debbie cried out in awe, completely forgetting to use her library voice. "There must be at least three dozen there!"

"Five," Eggers corrected in a clipped tone. "And they need to go home with you today."

"They're too pretty to be stuck back here anyway," Debbie said peevishly.

Lee ignored both of them and dug around frantically for a card or some other indication of who sent the flowers.

"Where's the card?" she demanded of her boss.

"There was no card," he said in a voice that sliced through the air. "They arrived anonymously."

Lee and Debbie looked at each other and shrugged. There was only one man Lee could think of who might have sent her flowers, and that was Paul. The gesture seemed a little extravagant for what she knew of him, and he and Lee hadn't dated very long, but there hadn't been anyone else recently. Except Roddy O'Neill, of course, and she knew that was just impossible.

Her brows together, she reached around the outsized bouquet for her phone, then punched out Paul's number. It would be nothing less than awkward to call him, but she had to know where the flowers had come from.

"Hi, Paul, it's Lee," she told him when he came on the line. "I'm sorry to bother you, but I just got a strange delivery, and I wondered if it was from you?"

Paul's tone was perplexed. "No. You told me you didn't want to see me anymore, remember?"

"So you didn't send me five dozen red roses?"

"Five doz—no. Maybe I should have, huh?"

Lee felt like a heel for even making the call, and she couldn't get Paul off the phone fast enough. Once she did, she turned to her boss again.

"Mr. Eggers," she said with a quaver in her tone, "are you sure these flowers are for me and not Debbie?"

He fixed her with the expected glare and raised his nose a notch. He hated to be doubted, particularly by his underlings. "Of course I'm sure."

Lee turned to helplessly regard the flowers again. She could forget about doing anything productive that afternoon. Even after moving the outsized bouquet so it no longer took up the entire top of her desk, wondering about its origins occupied her mind.

"If Paul didn't send them, who did?" Debbie asked several times that day.

Lee asked herself the same question. She was outgoing and social, but she did not have a string of admirers. Aside from a one-night stand with Roddy O'Neill, there hadn't been any other man in her life in months.

"Maybe it's the pizza delivery guy or your mailman," Debbie suggested. "They both like you."

"Maybe." Lee was certain Debbie was way off-base with the suggestion.

Debbie dared to mention the unmentionable again. "Do you think Roddy sent them?"

Lee emphatically shook her head. "Impossible. He doesn't even know my name. Besides, I'm sure he's forgotten me by now." Too bad she would never forget him.

It had occurred to her, of course, that he might have sent the flowers, but she dismissed the idea almost as quickly as it came to mind. Much as their night together meant to Lee, she knew Roddy did not feel the same. He had short little flings in strange cities all the time, so there was no reason to think there was anything special or particularly memorable about her.

The whole dilemma was giving her a headache, and Lee turned away from the flowers, determined not to think about them anymore. Her resolve lasted less than a minute.

ଔ

Over the next two months, Lee returned from lunch one day every week to find a huge bouquet of flowers towering over her desk. The day of the week always varied, as did the type of flowers, though they were always red. There was never a card indicating who sent them.

Mr. Eggers had given up harassing her about it weeks ago, and instead just tightened his lips and gave the flowers his patented disapproving stare. He no doubt wondered about young people in the modern world, and who would be crazy enough to send truckloads of flowers to a lowly library clerk.

Lee was becoming a bundle of anxiety. She had no idea who kept sending the extravagant bouquets every week, and it was starting to drive her crazy.

There was one thing she knew for certain: they weren't from Roddy. There was no way a man like him would think to send her flowers every week, even if he had bothered to figure out who she was. If it had happened only once, she might have allowed herself to entertain a small hope. Since it kept happening every week for two months, she was certain it must be someone else, like the pizza delivery guy. Roddy O'Neill certainly had better things to do than moon over her.

Lee found herself scrutinizing the strange men in her midst. Her admirer could be anyone, even some guy who rode her bus. None of them seemed to take any unusual interest, though. They just kept their noses buried in their newspapers as usual.

Lee broke down a little one afternoon in June when she found a regular forest of bleeding hearts decorating her desk when she and Debbie returned from lunch.

She simply stood in front of her desk and moaned. "I can't take this anymore."

"I wouldn't complain," Debbie said on a pout. "Nobody ever sends me flowers."

"There are enough here for six people! You'd think if someone was spending this much on flowers, he could at least spring for a card. You'd think he'd want me to know who he is!"

It was the last time she received flowers. The following week, Monday through Friday, her desk was empty every day when she returned from lunch. When there still had been no delivery by four o'clock Friday, Lee realized none would be forthcoming.

"I think he finally gave up on me," she murmured to Debbie, her feelings a mixture of disappointment and relief.

The words had no sooner left her mouth when Mr. Eggers loomed in the doorway.

"Miss Miller," he sniffed. "There is a gentleman out front who has asked specifically for your assistance." His tone suggested Mr. Eggers considered her visitor no gentleman.

Lee shrugged at Debbie, ordered herself to remain calm, then slid slowly away from her desk and followed Mr. Eggers out of the research department to meet the mysterious man who had asked specifically for her.

CHAPTER FIVE

MEANWHILE, OUT ON TOUR...

For the first time in as long as he could remember, Eddie left the party early. It had been a rocking party, too. Still, his overwhelming concern for his best friend drove him to dismiss a luscious young lady and leave her lovely promises unfulfilled.

Despite his concern, Eddie banged unceremoniously on Roddy's door. Roddy was wide awake, even at that ridiculous hour, and opened the door in his underwear. Eddie barged past him and settled himself in a chair, propping his booted feet on a table before saying a word.

"You okay, man?" he asked as he helped himself to one of Roddy's cigarettes.

Roddy dropped into another chair and gave him a quizzical look. "Yeah, why?"

"You've been different ever since we played that gig in Minneapolis," Eddie said through a haze of smoke. "You haven't been to an after party since. You just sit in your room by yourself."

"I'm burnt," was Roddy's explanation.

Eddie gave him a hard look. "Burned out on

women, too? You haven't brought anyone back to your room in two weeks."

Roddy sloshed whiskey into a pair of glasses before he responded. "I didn't see anything I liked."

"At least not since Minneapolis," Eddie remarked. "I mean, she was hot and everything, but…"

"Don't talk about her."

Eddie paused with his glass of whiskey only halfway to his mouth and fixed Roddy with a penetrating stare.

"Oh," he said at last. "You're still thinking about her? Jeez, Rod, you haven't done that since you were twenty." Eddie meant to give him a hard time about her, but somehow couldn't muster up the enthusiasm for it. Something was seriously afoot.

Roddy ran a hand over his face. "Just because I liked someone I slept with doesn't mean I'm doomed."

Eddie just smiled. "I don't know about that. You've spent almost all your time alone since you met her. I can't even remember the last time I saw you go outside."

"I've been writing," was Roddy's explanation, and he indicated a pile of papers under the guitarist's boot heel.

Eddie stretched forward and snatched up the papers, scattering ashes everywhere as he did so. Ignoring the mess, he read the lines Roddy had scrawled on the pages.

"This is pretty good," he remarked a few minutes later. He set the sheaf down and rose from his chair. "I think it could be better, though. I've got a couple ideas to spruce it up a little. I'll be right back."

Eddie returned to Roddy's room a few minutes later with an acoustic guitar. He sat down to show his bandmate what he had in mind, and in minutes, the two of them forgot the outside world as they collaborated on the song, as had happened so many times before. Roddy always started out with great material, and Eddie's input gave it the extra edge to turn the song into a chartbuster.

For the rest of that night, and for several nights following, Eddie holed up with Roddy in his hotel rooms so they could work on the song together. It was five o'clock in the morning when Roddy finally tossed down his pen and turned to Eddie with a smile.

"Let's find a studio and make a cut of this tomorrow," he suggested as he rubbed his eyes.

Eddie yawned hugely. "We'll be back in LA in a few weeks. It'll keep."

"I don't want to wait."

Eddie cracked open an eye and stared at Roddy with it. "Jeez, Rod. What's the rush? I haven't partied or met women in a week!"

"Oh, come on," Roddy cajoled. "Just one more day."

He looked startled when Eddie suddenly sat upright and leveled him with a stare.

"I'm not giving her another night, Roddy," he said firmly. "I've lost enough sleep over some woman who doesn't even like me." When Roddy looked like he was going to protest, Eddie waved him back down. "You don't give me enough credit, my friend. I remember when you picked her up at the backstage party in Minneapolis. Maybe you don't think I pay attention, but I do. I notice a lot more than I let on."

"And sometimes even stuff that isn't there," Roddy grumbled, getting defensive.

Eddie told himself to tread carefully. They had both been subsisting on very little sleep for several days, and they were both short-tempered. It probably wasn't the best time to needle his friend, but he couldn't just let it go.

"Okay, I'm sure I'm imagining things. Just because you wrote that song doesn't mean it's about her, right?"

"It's not the first time I've written a song about a woman." Roddy's tone was defensive.

"No, but it's the first time the word love has been in it eighteen times, not including the chorus."

Roddy groaned. "Go to bed, Eddie. You're losing it."

Eddie grabbed his guitar and tried not to grin too much on his way out. He wasn't sure what was suddenly making his best friend act so different, but he really hadn't been the same since the blonde in Minneapolis. That Roddy was touchy about her spoke volumes, and Eddie wasn't even going to mention the rest of the lyrics to the new song.

Life was sure getting interesting.

ଔ

It seemed all hell had waited for Roddy to finish writing his song before breaking loose. In one week's time, he had two television interviews in Chicago and three radio shows in other cities along the tour. As if that wasn't enough, Zeke's lawyer telephoned him one day to announce that some girl in Florida was slapping his bandmate with a paternity suit. Mike got arrested for disturbing the peace in Kansas City. Then, just when things seemed to be cooling off and it looked like they might be able to finish the tour in some sort of peace, Dana McMillan showed up in his doorway.

Dana was an old flame Roddy had been glad to extinguish several years ago. She was a professional model and as narcissistic as they come. Roddy had gotten involved with her in the first place because his manager told him it would be good for his image to be linked with someone like her. It was Roddy's own fault he indulged in an affair with Dana shortly after they made their acquaintance, and he had cause to regret it almost immediately. From the moment the paparazzi got wind of their relationship, not a day went by that Roddy didn't have a camera in his face or trying to get into his bedroom. When, in the end, Roddy finally decided to end his association with her, his face appeared on every tabloid in the country, accompanied by untrue stories of his emotional and physical abuse.

Dana McMillan brought back anything but pleasant memories, but now here she was, standing in his doorway in the tightest dress Roddy had ever seen.

Unmoved by his less than enthusiastic greeting, Dana flung her arms around his neck, knocking his bandanna askew. She knew he hated to have his bandanna messed with, but as usual, his feelings weren't part of the equation with her.

"Oh, Roddy!" she squealed, smearing lipstick on his cheek as she backed away about an inch. "It's so good to see you again!"

"Dana." He pushed her away with unnecessary force and scrubbed at his face with the heel of his hand. "What did I do to deserve this?"

"Come on, Roddy," she said on a purr. "You know you need the publicity as much as I do."

That wasn't exactly true, as Roddy was already on television at least once a week, the band's San Francisco concert was airing on pay-per-view that month, and, at the moment, his face was on the cover of just about every trade publication that counted. Any more exposure for Roddy would have crossed the line into exploitation, so he knew Dana must be desperate for some media attention of her own.

He was unsurprised a moment later when Dana suddenly draped herself over him just long enough for a photographer to appear and snap a very cozy picture. He was sure it would appear in the tabloids within days, accompanied by a false story of their reconciliation.

Roddy managed to extricate himself from Dana rather quickly that day, but she kept appearing everywhere he went for the next week, and finally Roddy had had enough.

"Get that bitch away from me," he muttered to Eddie when he saw her headed his way.

Eddie seemingly pulled a shapely blonde out of thin air and made the introductions before Dana could approach.

"Greta, meet Roddy O'Neill," he said with a flourish to the startled blonde. "He's been watching you all night and asked me to make the introductions."

Greta recovered amazingly well and quickly attached herself to Roddy like Velcro. Roddy wasn't thrilled with the situation, but he supposed it was better than being photographed with Dana again.

The next day, Roddy was on the cover of a tabloid smiling into Greta's incredible blue eyes. The accompanying story cattily informed the world that Roddy had thrown over the luscious Dana McMillan for a Swedish college student and, in retaliation, Dana had taken up with Eddie. It didn't help Roddy's mood any that part of the story was true.

Roddy had really given it his best with Greta, but even the ethereally beautiful young woman couldn't hold his attention. That was apparently still with his library clerk back in Minneapolis, so after a couple of hours of being photographed with Greta at the party, he extricated himself from her, as well.

Irritated with the world at large, Roddy took out all his frustration on the band. Eddie, as tired of everything as Roddy by then, finally made him lose his temper. One night in a bar, words came to blows, and in seconds they were rolling around on the floor, getting their photographs taken. Roddy and Eddie were laughing again by the time their bodyguards pulled them apart, and he supposed both of them had needed the release of throwing a few halfhearted punches at each other.

"You know what this means, don't you?" he said

to Eddie as they knocked a couple of friendly beers together.

"Yeah, our record stays at number one for another week!" Eddie roared on a laugh before he sucked down his entire beer and loudly ordered another round.

It was true, and Roddy found himself finally able to let go of some frustrations. Wasn't it better to laugh and roll with it? This wasn't the band's first long, grueling tour, and they were always fraught with tensions and stress. Roddy wasn't sure why he was so uptight this time around, but it felt good to let loose at last.

The tour finally wrapped up two weeks later, and the band was in high spirits. Roddy gave everybody a month off to relax and go their separate ways before rehearsals would begin for the next go-around. As expected, Eddie would return to his home in the Hollywood hills and the woman there who posed as his girlfriend. The rest of the band scattered in several directions.

"What's in the cards for you, Rod?" Eddie asked over breakfast one morning as they sat in a diner sipping coffee.

"I think I'm going to head for Minnesota. I hear the weather is nice up there this time of year." Roddy tried to sound casual, to no avail.

"You son of a bitch," Eddie said on a laugh. "You're going back to her. Even after I introduced you to Greta!"

"You can have Greta and her ilk," Roddy grumbled. "I wanted to kill you for passing her off on me. There wasn't nearly enough of a language barrier."

"I thought she was just what you needed," Eddie said defensively.

"Like another hole in the head." Roddy grimaced. "I don't think I've ever been happier to see the end of a tour."

"I hear you," Eddie agreed vehemently. "Now finish your coffee so we can get out of here. Claire awaits."

"Claire. I can't believe you're still keeping her around. She's dumber than a stump."

Eddie cracked his now-famous grin. "Just the way I like 'em!"

ଔ

Roddy didn't want to examine his reasons for returning to Minneapolis too closely. Naturally, he was going back for Lee, but was it just because he desperately needed to see her again, or because he needed to assure himself she was no different than any of the other women he'd met in the two months since he had seen her? He supposed if he had the answer to that question, he wouldn't be making the long drive from Los Angeles to Minneapolis, to the address where he had figured out she worked.

He could have flown, of course, but Roddy liked to drive, and he needed to clear his head. He couldn't think of a better method of doing so than pushing his Maserati past 100 miles an hour every chance he got along the way.

Even when he was minding his own business, Roddy couldn't avoid publicity, though. When he got a speeding ticket in Kansas, it made the evening entertainment news and a quick spot on MTV. Wryly, he noticed it helped his record stay at number one.

It seemed an eternity had passed since he had last beheld the Minneapolis skyline. Seeing it again, he realized he was finally only minutes away from the woman who had haunted his dreams for two months. It made him feel sixteen again, the way he felt after he played his first high school dance so long ago, and that brought a smile to his lips. He had the feeling this trip to Minneapolis would also have a major impact on his life, and his foot pressed harder on the accelerator in anticipation.

CHAPTER SIX

Lee's heart leapt to her throat when she saw Roddy in the library, casually leaned against a magazine rack. The library didn't get many visits from men wearing custom-made white leather pants that fit like a second skin. Lee also knew she would have recognized his rattlesnake boots anywhere. Roddy's hair was caught under a bandanna tied over the top of his head, and when he smiled at her, she thought he looked good enough to eat.

One thought kept reverberating through her mind: he was there for her.

She had a few seconds to drink in the sight of him before he noticed her, and she felt a warm rush as she watched him flipping carelessly through an issue of *Rolling Stone*.

"Hello," she said a bit unsteadily on her approach. "May I help you?"

In response, Roddy set aside the magazine in seeming slow motion and then sauntered up to her, stopping just inches away. He frowned, and Lee wondered what was wrong until he wordlessly reached up behind her and set her hair free from the severe bun in which she'd had it confined.

"That's better," he said with a smile. "It's a crime to hide such beautiful hair."

Lee knew she should have been outraged at the gesture, but found herself smiling back instead.

He gave her a long, slow appraisal, taking in her prim white blouse and knee-length gray skirt. He finally said, "You look different."

"Like a librarian?"

He smiled. "Yeah. I like your green jacket better."

"You look just the same," Lee found her voice again to say.

His wry grin tore at her heartstrings. "Goes with the job. I get to wear whatever I want."

They just stood there, smiling stupidly at each other, completely at a loss for words for several long seconds.

"It was you all along," Lee finally said to break the silence.

"What, the flowers?"

"Of course."

He smiled devilishly. "Nope, that wasn't me. Must've been someone else."

She smiled back. "How did you find me?"

"I have my ways."

"You really had me going with the flowers. I never would have thought in a million years it was you. I can't believe you even remembered me, and I didn't even tell you my name."

"I know." Roddy's voice was soft, and his eyes intense.

Lee stared back, curious. "How did you find me out?"

He shrugged. "I cheated." He pulled her much-handled deposit slip out of his shirt pocket.

Lee frowned and took a step back, after snatching the offending slip of paper out of his fingers.

"You went through my purse!" The accusation lacked amusement of any kind.

Roddy seemed shocked by her reaction, no doubt unused to women who complained about anything he did.

"I'm sorry," he said simply. "Are you more upset I had to go through your purse, or that I found out who you are?"

That took the wind out of her sails, and Lee felt a little thrill creeping into her belly.

"I can't believe you'd do that."

"You wouldn't tell me your name."

"And you really cared to know it?"

Roddy frowned slightly. "Of course I did. Why wouldn't I? It really started to bug me that you were being so secretive about yourself. You were sleeping, so I just looked in the most obvious place. I didn't snoop through anything else."

"Do you always do whatever you want?"

He shrugged but looked a little perturbed. "I guess I do."

Lee had to laugh at the contrite expression on his face, and her anger completely melted away. She gave him a warm smile.

"Is this for real?" she asked.

Roddy took her hands in his. "I sure hope so." He smiled back.

Lee realized he was about to kiss her, in front of

Mr. Eggers and everyone else in the library. She also knew she wouldn't have stopped him if Mr. Eggers hadn't suddenly stepped in. Belatedly, she realized he had been watching their entire exchange with avid distaste.

"Sir, is there anything I can assist you with this afternoon?" he asked stiffly, approaching from behind Lee's objectionable visitor.

Roddy turned and gave him a smile. "I think I have everything I need right here." He laid a proprietary hand on Lee's shoulder. "I'd like to check her out for the weekend."

"We'll need your library card," Mr. Eggers said automatically, before his mind fully processed Roddy's request. When both Roddy and Lee looked amused, he puffed up angrily.

"I think I can handle the paperwork," Lee said on a smile.

She tried to keep her amusement to herself, but obviously wasn't doing a very good job of it, since Eggers stiffened up some more. She was afraid of what might happen next, as Roddy didn't seem to care much about library rules and etiquette, and didn't seem willing to back down from a challenge from her boss.

Eggers surprised her with a tight smile. "You've worked awfully hard this week, Lee," he said. "Why don't you go home a little early today so you can spend some time with your visitor."

He appeared eager to get Roddy and his leather out of the library.

Lee still couldn't quite believe Roddy had come

back to Minneapolis just to see her. Their night together came rushing back, and it was obvious Roddy fondly remembered it, too. The chemistry between them was as strong as ever. He had a twinkle in his eye when he stared at her, and it was all she could do to recall where she was.

She forced herself to remember her manners and smile gratefully at Mr. Eggers. "Thank you. I'll just go get my things and we'll be off."

"Take your time," Roddy told her. "There's no need to rush, and I'd like to see more of the library."

Mr. Eggers did not look pleased by the announcement, and Lee chuckled to herself as she left them alone to rush back to Research and Cataloging.

Debbie seemed excited when Lee walked in.

"Lee, take a look outside!" she commanded from her post near the window. "There's a Maserati out there."

"I know. It's Roddy's." Lee strove to keep her voice calm, but already felt it rising before Debbie turned to give her an incredulous stare. "He's here."

"Roddy O'Neill? He's *here*?" Debbie knocked a stack of books onto the floor as she raced across the room to enfold Lee in a bear hug. "I knew he sent those flowers!"

Lee hugged her back for a second, but quickly pulled away. "Eggers is letting me go early, but I think he just wants to get Roddy out of the library. He's wearing leather pants and a bandanna, and one of his tattoos is showing."

"Oh my god!" Debbie laughed. "Eggers must be having a heart attack. What are you doing standing around back here talking to me? Go have some fun with your man!"

※

I can't believe this is really happening to me, Lee thought with glee as water streamed off her head and washed over her body.

While she took her customary after-work shower, Roddy O'Neill, the world-famous rock star, was sitting in her living room with her furniture, photos, and books. It was possible he had ventured into other parts of her apartment and probably even noticed what a mess her bedroom was. She supposed it didn't matter what her apartment looked like. The important thing was that Roddy O'Neill was in it. She still couldn't quite believe her luck.

Once again, her life seemed to have slipped the confines of reality. For the second time now, she wasn't just Lee Miller, the dull library clerk who wore no-nonsense skirts and boring sweaters to work. With Roddy, she became a sexy, desirable woman capable of bringing the hero of millions back to her from thousands of miles away.

Lee didn't want to examine the reasons why Roddy had driven all the way from California to see her. She didn't want to worry about where things were going. For now, she was living in the present, and she would continue to do so for as long as Roddy O'Neill was there. It wasn't likely they would have a future of any kind, so she needed to enjoy what she had in hand.

Annoyed that her thoughts had even gone down that road when she really should just be enjoying herself, Lee sternly shut off the shower and wiped water from her eyes. She flung back the shower curtain and reached blindly out to pluck her towel off the counter.

It wasn't there.

Instead, Roddy was perched on the edge of the counter where the towel was supposed to be. Admiration for her wet, naked body gleamed in his eyes.

Lee's first impulse was to shriek and jump back into the tub with the shower curtain to cover her. She tamped down on it, though, and forced herself to smile boldly at him instead. This was Roddy O'Neill, a man who freely admitted he did whatever he pleased. Apparently, she pleased him a lot at the moment, and she couldn't find it in herself to complain.

"Nothing on TV?" she asked saucily as she stood there, like having a rock star in her bathroom was an everyday thing.

"It's more interesting in here," he murmured as he handed her the towel.

She took it, careful not to appear too hasty, and applied it to her wet hair. Out of the corner of her eye, she saw Roddy slipping out of his boots. She stilled and held the towel in front of her body.

"I can get you another towel if you want a shower," she suggested helpfully.

"Don't need one," he said, kicking his boots aside and coming toward her in his socks, which were fast getting soaked with all the water Lee dripped onto the floor.

He removed the towel from her suddenly uncertain fingers and flung it over his shoulder. Then he picked her up and carried her down the hall to her bedroom.

"I took the liberty of finding out where all the important stuff is in this place," he informed her while she caught her breath. "I hope you don't mind."

Once in her bedroom, he set her on the bed, then pushed her gently onto her back. He kissed her once before rolling them over so she was on top of him.

"Take my pants off," he husked in her ear.

Operating on sheer instinct, Lee fumbled with the laces while his hands roamed softly over her body. Once Roddy's pants were loosened, he rolled back over so Lee was beneath him again. He rose onto his knees to tug his pants down and yanked his shirt over his head, then tossed it over his shoulder with the same carelessness he had shown Lee's towel. Then he paused to simply stare at her.

No words were necessary between them. There was only the hunger and need they had both denied for so many weeks. Frantic hands and ravenous mouths met heated skin as they gave and took. Their bodies seemed built solely for each other, like two parts of a whole that had been deprived of one another for far too long. They came together with a driving need that was almost violent.

Afterwards, Roddy cradled her gently in his arms while he took deep, ragged breaths. If Lee wasn't mistaken, he seemed just as swept away by this thing between them as she was.

She lay there staring at the ceiling in the gathering darkness and bit her lip. It seemed unbelievable this had started as a simple, unfulfilled crush on a rock star. Her first night with Roddy had been surreal, a night excluded from time. Not once had she allowed herself the tiniest hope that he would come back for her. She certainly didn't think a man like Roddy O'Neill needed to drive halfway across the country just for good sex. So why had he come all the way back? What did it mean for her future? Was there any way at all they could have a future?

She forced her voice to sound light and careless when their breathing slowed and she finally spoke. "How was the rest of the tour?"

"Sheer hell," he grumbled into his pillow. "I've never seen so many publicity stunts. I suppose it's good for record sales, though."

"Like Dana McMillan?" Lee couldn't resist bringing up the model. She at least needed to understand Roddy's relationship with the other woman.

"Dana McMillan isn't good for anything," Roddy told her flatly. "Just to preserve my reputation, I'll have you know I had the good sense to finish with her years ago. All those photos were faked."

"I wondered why you'd come to see me if she was waiting for you. I mean, she's so beautiful and famous."

"Also shallow, empty-headed, and vain, and I'm sick of talking about her already."

Roddy looked decidedly unhappy to be discussing an ex-lover while in another woman's bed. He sat up and pushed the sheets away, then rose to his feet with a stretch. Lee admired his naked body while he hunted around on the floor for his clothes, but didn't know what to say when Roddy left the room in search of her bathroom again.

She regretted bringing up Dana McMillan now. Lee realized she didn't know Roddy well enough to grill him about other women in his life, and hoped he wasn't upset with her.

He was smiling when he came back to her bedroom with his clothes on a few minutes later. He perched on the bed next to her and asked, "Are you hungry?"

"Sort of," she said, unsure of herself now.

Roddy ran a hand through his hair and smiled. "Just like a woman to be 'sort of' hungry when I'm starving half to death."

Lee looked away. "I'm sorry. I don't have much food in the house. I'm single, so…"

"Maybe you can tell me about somewhere else to get a decent meal in this town," Roddy suggested.

She thought for a moment. "I know there are some good restaurants on Lyndale."

Roddy took her hands gently in his and gave them a squeeze. "I don't want directions," he said. "I want to take you out."

Lee turned bright pink. "Oh."

Roddy gave her a lopsided smile. "I guess I need to work on my reputation a little. You always seem to think the worst of me. First you thought I was going to kick you out of my hotel room, and now you think I want to leave already? I didn't drive all the way here to spend a half hour in your bed, though it *was* worth it." Roddy sobered for a moment. "Unless you want me to go?"

"No!" Lee exclaimed, feeling even worse now for making him think she didn't want him there when he had driven all the way from Los Angeles just to see her. She wasn't handling anything very well, and strove to fix it. "I just thought you got upset when I mentioned Dana, and…"

"Forget it," he said, looking down at her with a smile. "Now, are you going to just lie there looking lovely while I starve to death, or are you going to get out of bed so you can take me somewhere for some food? I'm very hungry."

They opted for a huge, cheesy pizza at an Italian place just a few blocks away. Roddy seemed at home there, and none of the waiters or other patrons seemed to recognize him, or if they did, they were discreet.

"This place was great after some of the greasy spoons we stopped at on tour," Roddy told Lee on their way out of the restaurant. "What else is there to do in this town?"

It was a beautiful summer evening with lots of possibilities, but Lee didn't know what rock stars did for fun, so she said, "Not much."

"I was hoping you'd say that," he said with a grin. "I'm a little tired after the drive and all."

"And I keep forgetting things like that. You must think I'm so inconsiderate." Lee looked up at him with contrition. "I can let you go back to your hotel and get some rest."

To her surprise, Roddy scowled again and their easy stroll down the sidewalk halted. He slowly backed her up against the brick wall of the restaurant and pinned her there with his hips and his eyes. He was firm without seeming aggressive, but Lee's eyes widened a bit in shock. She struggled against his hands for a moment when they gripped her upper arms, but stopped when his hips pressed into hers more firmly.

"Let's get something straight," he said, all seriousness. "I'm plenty capable of telling you to kiss off if I want to, and don't think I've never done it to anyone before. I'm here for *you*, and nothing else, so while I'm here, I want to be with you. I drove all the way from LA because for some reason, I haven't been able to get you off my mind. And now, I get the feeling you want me to leave. Is that what you want? Because if it is, I'm gone."

There was the slightest catch in his last word that zapped Lee right in the gut. She supposed it stood to reason that he really had been thinking that much about her, considering all the flowers he sent. It was hard to think of Roddy O'Neill in the same way she thought of other men because of who he was, but Lee realized that under the fame, he was just a man.

She didn't know what to say, so she simply reached for him. Her hands softly came up to frame his face and, without even bumping his bandanna, she pulled his mouth down to hers. Her kiss was gentle and giving, yet at the same time held some of the fire she felt for him. He responded in kind. His hands on her shoulders moved to the back of her head and buried themselves in her hair. As his hips ground hers roughly against the wall, both of them forgot where they were for a moment.

When Roddy finally pulled back, Lee met his eyes. "I'm sorry, Roddy," she told him. "I've been acting like an idiot, but you have to see things from my point of view. You're a rock star and I'm nobody, and stuff like this doesn't happen to me every day."

Something flared in his eyes, but he just smiled and took one of her hands in his. "Come on. I booked us a nice hotel suite before I found you at work. Why don't we go back there and hang out for the rest of the weekend?"

"I don't have anything else to wear."

"You won't need anything."

ଓ

Later, when Roddy's desire for her had been temporarily sated, he ordered up room service so they could eat in front of the TV.

"I could get fat if I spent much time with you," Lee remarked.

"And I'd just be exhausted," Roddy said on a laugh. "If we keep this up, I'm going to have to take more vitamins."

She looked him over slowly. "I didn't know you were a health nut."

"I'm not, but my mother is always after me to take my vitamins," he said on a grin. "She's afraid I'm going to die of scurvy or something."

"I take it you're close?" Lee asked while her fingers absently stroked the tattoo on his upper left arm.

"Yeah." His voice turned husky.

Roddy glanced down at her leisurely exploration of his skin and felt an almost overwhelming wave of warmth steal over him. What was his problem? His body responded like a fifteen-year-old's to her slightest touch. When he should be exhausted and lying limply in the tangled sheets, her fingers on his arm were doing wild things to his pulse. Women with impressive skills had tried much harder to get a response from him with disappointing results, but all Lee had to do was look at him and he wanted her.

She jerked his attention back to the present with a question. "What's your mother like?"

"She's great," he answered with a smile. "She's just a—a mom, you know? She bought me my first guitar and then started parking her car in the driveway so I could use the garage to practice."

"How come you never play guitar on stage?"

He ruffled her hair a little. "I'm not all that good. Certainly can't touch Eddie. I can get by, but my main talent is singing. I didn't get a recording contract until I put down my guitar."

"But you still take it with you wherever you go?"

"I like to mess around with it in my downtime, and I use it when I'm working on new songs."

"You didn't mention a father."

"He died when I was little. I barely remember him. So, what about your family?"

Lee sighed and rolled onto her back, staring up at the ceiling for several seconds before answering. Obviously, talking about her family was not one of her favorite things.

"My father lives in Minneapolis, but we don't see

each other much," she said at last. "I have no idea where my mother is."

"Do you want to?"

She shrugged. "Sometimes, when I've felt like he drove her away and she had to leave me behind for some secret reason she couldn't say, I have wanted to find her. But, deep down, I know she never would have left me if she really wanted to be my mother, so I leave it alone."

"That's pretty sad," Roddy told her candidly.

Lee snorted. "If you say so. But my life doesn't revolve around *her*. Or my father. I'm kind of on my own, and I have friends."

"Like the girl at the concert?"

"Debbie? Yeah, she's a pretty good friend."

"And boyfriends?"

Lee shrugged. "Here and there, but nobody serious."

"Why not?"

She hid her eyes with her lashes. "Never met the right guy, I guess."

"Hmm."

Lee inched closer to him, fascinated again with his tattoos. The one on his left arm was a stylized sea monster, and after she ran a finger over the outline, she leaned over him so she could check out the one on his right. That one showed a heart with an arrow embedded in it, and a drop of blood beneath.

"These are really cool," she remarked.

"You like tattoos?"

"Not as a rule, no. But yours seem to suit you. I can't imagine you without them."

"I think my mother gave up the dream of having a normal kid the day I came home with this one," he chuckled, covering her hand with his over the heart tattoo. "She just shook her head and started praying for me."

Lee laughed softly, her lips brushing his knuckles. He moved his hand to stroke her hair, so she started to kiss his tattoo.

Nobody had really ever done that before. Though women always told him they liked his tattoos, up close, they tended to shy away from them as if they were contagious. Lee, who claimed not to care much for body art, kissed his arm almost worshipfully, which managed to drive him crazy on more than one level.

When she finished with his right arm, her lips moved softly across his chest and began the same ministrations on his left.

Roddy felt the sensations taking him under again and tried to restart their conversation. "Do you have any other friends besides Debbie?"

"A couple, but no one else I'm close to like her. I guess I'm kind of self-contained and private." Lee's lips made a trail across his chest, punctuating her words with soft kisses as she made her way back to his neck, and then moved down toward his navel.

"Private, but quite personable," Roddy murmured, a hand catching in her hair.

Roddy couldn't understand Lee's response once she reached her destination, but he suddenly lost all interest in conversation.

CHAPTER SEVEN

The following morning, Lee was awakened by a discreet knock from room service. She cracked her eyes open wide enough to watch Roddy go to the door in nothing but a pair of white cotton pants hanging low on his hips. He opened the door and stood back while the waiter wheeled a cart into the room, then gave the man what looked like a generous tip before closing the door behind him again.

Roddy pushed the cart up to the bed and lifted the cover off a plate of bacon. The smell wafted to Lee's nostrils and mingled with the scent of steaming coffee he poured. Lee yawned and stretched, then finally fully opened her eyes to confront Roddy's.

"Good morning," he rumbled in a voice that sounded as sleepy as she felt.

"Do you ever sleep?"

"Not much," he admitted with a smile as he seated himself on the bed beside her. "I hope you're hungry. I ordered lots of food."

"Actually, I'm famished."

"Good. Eat up and then we're going shopping."

"Shopping? I thought men hated shopping."

He cocked an eyebrow. "And I thought women loved it."

"That's beside the point. Why do you want to take me shopping?"

He gave her a slow, wicked grin. "I get the feeling you're trying to keep me locked up in this hotel room. Don't you ever need to see the sunlight, or are you some sort of vampire?"

"A vampire? There aren't any marks on your neck."

"Not on my neck, but I thought I saw a couple tooth marks on the inside of my thigh."

"What!" Lee was mortified. She was able to be rather uninhibited with him, but she honestly couldn't remember having bitten him.

Roddy laughed and rolled on top of her. "You should see the look on your face. It's priceless. Don't worry, Lee. I was joking." His lips nibbled at her ear. "But you can bite me anywhere you want any time."

◊

The intimate camaraderie between them lasted all day, even when Roddy insisted on buying her a dress at a downtown department store. It was a beautiful garment, but the style was a bit more daring than what Lee usually wore, and the price tag was outrageous. She had never worn anything worth more than a week's pay before.

"I can afford it," Roddy said flippantly when she objected.

"You'll make me feel like a kept woman," she argued.

He stared into her eyes for a moment. "Would that be so bad?" He waited a beat and then added, "Besides, one little dress hardly qualifies."

"Little sums it up nicely."

"The librarian in you is showing."

That remark was all it took. Lee did work in a library, but it didn't mean she was dull and frumpy. She wasn't completely comfortable with it, but she let Roddy buy the dress.

He insisted she must have shoes to match, and when she suggested she could pick some up at her apartment, he refused to take her home. Once again, she gave into his wheedling charm and allowed him to buy the shoes, too. That they were gorgeous, strappy sandals in iridescent peacock blue didn't hurt in the decision-making process, but the fact that they cost almost as much as the dress made her bite her lip.

"Do you always do this for women?" Lee couldn't resist asking as they walked out of the store.

"No."

"Why not?"

"Because they expect me to."

The answer was so calm and matter-of-fact, Lee took him at his word. She knew nothing about his day-to-day life, and found herself intensely curious about it, but still afraid to pry. Despite the chemistry between them, and the way he acted so natural with her, Lee still could not forget he was a millionaire rock star. It seemed so unreal that he was even there, she found herself just going along for the ride. She would sort out what everything meant later.

Lee offered to take him to the Mall of America,

but Roddy made a face and told her everyone wanted to see the Mall when they came to Minneapolis. He wanted to see other things, so she took him on a drive around the city's three premier lakes, then they parked the Maserati and wandered through nearby Calhoun Square and the rest of Uptown. They ate dinner at a restaurant there, and emerged when the sun was dipping toward the western horizon.

"What kind of night life do they have in this town?" Roddy wanted to know.

Lee balked. She didn't sit home with six cats every night, but she also lacked the means to enjoy a glittering night life. She occasionally shared a beer at a corner bar with Debbie, and from time to time they went to a nightclub, but she hardly felt qualified to take Roddy out for a night on the town.

"I'm not really up on the hot spots," she told him. "But we could troll a few of the nightclubs downtown."

Roddy frowned. "Hmm. We could, but I might get recognized. Minnesotans are pretty mellow about stuff like that, but I'd still rather not go through that right now."

"Okay." Lee thought for a moment, and finally decided to take him to a little place she occasionally visited on Lake Street. It was kind of a dive, but when she explained, Roddy just smiled.

"That sounds perfect. Do they have a dance floor?"

"A small one. Are you sure you want to go there? It's not the best place. There have been fights in there before."

He fixed her with a look. "Haven't you figured out yet that I'm not a nice boy?"

She smiled a little at that. "Okay, if you're sure. But don't blame me if something happens."

Roddy gave her another odd glance. "I just got through several months of utter craziness, and I've been in some bars I wouldn't even drive past with you. Come to think of it, I even got into a couple fights. So…if something happens tonight, I doubt if it'll be your fault."

Lee couldn't argue with that.

"Besides you, there is only one other person on earth who knows where I am right now," Roddy went on. "I can't tell you how nice that feels. I'd kind of like to keep a low profile, so I'll try not to start anything, okay?"

"Okay." Lee paused a beat. "Only one other person knows where you are?"

"Yup."

"So she'll come after me if anything happens to you."

Roddy smirked. "He. And I don't think Eddie would hold you accountable."

ೞ

On Lee's advice, Roddy parked his Maserati back in the ramp at their hotel and they took a cab to the bar on Lake Street. He sat admiring Lee in the backseat all the way there. She was a lot of fun for a librarian. He could tell that under her practical, Minnesota girl exterior lurked a woman who wasn't afraid to experience life to the fullest, no matter what that entailed. He actually admired the way she tried

CALIFORNIA DREAM

to suppress that part of herself, though. Too many women he knew thought experiencing life to the fullest meant grabbing everything in reach without discretion, but Lee had once again proven she was different.

He also admired the way she looked in her new dress. It hugged her body and stopped several inches above her knees. Even if she hadn't told him, he would have guessed she didn't usually wear such revealing clothes. The fact that she wasn't afraid to impressed him. She wore the sexy dress with style and grace, not fidgeting or tugging on the hemline.

He was already in love with her hair. He could get lost in it. It was thick and lustrous, and tumbled in disarray down her back when she was still, softly swung when she walked, and he was able to think about little else but the way it had whipped around her head in abandon when they were in bed. He remembered the way her hair had brushed across his chest to softly stroke his skin with her every movement. Then he recalled the glimpse he had caught of her face through the blonde curtain. Her skin had been flushed, covered with a light sheen of perspiration, and little tendrils of hair had stuck to her in a very provocative way.

Roddy reached out to trap a lock of it between his fingers, enjoying the silky way it slipped through his grasp.

"What are you smiling about?" Lee asked.

"Nothing," he lied. "I was just admiring your hair."

"I've thought about cutting it all off."

"Don't you dare!"

Secretly, Roddy liked women with hair longer than his, and it wasn't always easy to find them.

Their cab pulled up in front of a little hole-in-the-wall bar on a busy, four-lane street, and Roddy smiled. It didn't look like a rough joint, in his opinion, and he doubted Lee would even know where to find such a place. The neighborhood it was in was not upscale, but it was also far from the ghetto. Still, Lee reached for his hand when they alighted from the cab, and Roddy pulled her close. He would enjoy being her protector.

Was there anything about her that he didn't enjoy?

She stayed by his side as they walked inside and up to the bar, but she ordered for herself instead of turning sea-green eyes to him and asking him to order for her. She sipped her drink and preceded Roddy to a corner table, scanning the bar with her eyes on the way. She seemed relaxed, and ignored the other men there, who all appeared to be dressed in a uniform of jeans, western shirts, and some sort of boots. None of them seemed overly fond of regular bathing, and Roddy wondered how Lee had come to be familiar with the establishment.

While she ignored the bar's other patrons, they all took avid notice of her. Roddy scowled at several other men who looked her over on their way to the table, and when he asked her to dance with him on the tiny patch of floor, he was sure every eye in the place was on them.

"I seem to be the only woman in here tonight," she remarked.

"I noticed that. Is it always like that here?"

"I don't know. I don't come very often. Usually just if there's a band."

The music that night was not to Roddy's taste, and guessed it wasn't Lee's, either. It was twangy country-western with topics that centered around drinking, pick-up trucks, and exes, and he amused himself mingling some of the concepts with his own music in his head.

"You look like you're having fun," Lee told him when she caught him smiling.

"I'm with you, aren't I?" he asked, spinning her in a fast circle before she could respond, and then giving her a quick dip before pulling her up against his chest.

He couldn't read the look in her eyes when they met his. Her face was flushed and her lips slightly parted, body molded casually against his while he turned her around the floor. He found himself wordlessly staring at her while they swayed to the music.

Lee finally broke the spell when she asked, "Have you ever thought about cutting off your hair?"

"Should I?"

"No! I love your hair."

"You can't be serious. Even Eddie hates it."

She frowned a little. "Really? So why do you wear it like that?"

"Because I like it."

"Well, so do I." A hand stole up, and she gave it a tug.

He moved in just a little closer. "I actually believe you, Lee. Most women just say things like that because they think they should, but I get the feeling you don't say things you don't mean."

Her body responded instantaneously to his husky words, and something in the way she held herself against him became more intimate. "I would never be dishonest with you. I feel like I can really be myself with you, in a way I've never been able to be with anyone else."

Roddy noticed that only their hips seemed to be moving against each other by that time. Their feet barely shuffled along, movement more of a suggestion than an actual thing. He felt an urge to grasp her by the nape of the neck and kiss her right then and there, but he controlled himself and murmured in her ear that they should sit back down and have another drink.

He led her to the lopsided table in the corner and stroked her bare thigh while they waited for a waitress to saunter over. He was glad nobody in the little bar seemed to recognize him, but he supposed that would stand to reason since it was a country joint, and he wondered if Lee had chosen it for that reason. The unusual anonymity made him feel reckless and free.

He noted that they were being eyed by another customer from across the room. The man's eyes lit on Lee with appreciation and then slid over Roddy, sizing him up. Roddy was sure the guy was thinking he was just some punk out trying to impress his pretty girlfriend. He wasn't exactly huge at just under six feet, and he wasn't bulky at all. Some reporters had even called him skinny. The other guy probably thought he was an easy mark, and proved the theory when he lurched out of his chair and headed their way.

"Do you mind if I dance with your lady?" the guy asked with a slight drunken slur to his words.

Roddy was about to tell him to piss off when Lee's head swung around and her eyes shot sparks.

"Whether or not he minds, maybe I'm the one you should ask," she snapped.

Roddy's eyes widened. He hadn't expected such a reaction from Lee, but supposed he should have known she wouldn't behave like a simpering, helpless female just because he was there. She was obviously used to taking care of herself.

The drunk smiled and tried to reach for her hand. "Let's dance, honey."

Lee's mild irritation crossed into anger as she recoiled. "No thanks."

"Spunky, aren't you?"

Lee didn't deign to answer. Her eyes had gone frosty, and her posture stiff. She appeared ready to strike.

"Go away," Roddy said to the man in a low, conversational tone.

The drunk turned his attention away from Lee to look Roddy up and down. Only the fact that Lee wasn't used to his rowdy lifestyle had stopped him from punching the guy already.

The drunk turned on him. "Did you say something to me?"

Roddy stood and his chair crashed into the wall. "I said go away. She's with me, and she doesn't want you bothering her anymore. Get lost before I hurt you."

The drunk staggered and laughed heartily at that. "Hurt me? A wimp like you?"

Roddy lost his temper and saw red. His arm went back, fist prepared to smash into the other man's jaw, when Lee suddenly popped up between them.

Her fingers curled over his fist and she leaned into him to murmur in his ear. "You don't need this kind of publicity right now," she reminded him, meeting his eyes.

He didn't give a damn about the publicity. What he wanted was to enjoy a nice, peaceful evening with Lee, without any drunken idiots getting in the way, but he knew it wasn't going to happen if he got into a fight. Only for that reason did he subside.

"That's more like it," the obnoxious oaf sneered when Roddy relaxed.

Lee suddenly turned on him and stomped on his toe with the heel of a new strappy sandal. "Get lost!" she snarled in his face.

The bartender finally chose that moment to realize there was a problem in his establishment, and reacted in typical fashion: he blamed Lee.

"Hey, buster," he yelled at Roddy, startling the reeling drunk, who whipped his head around to stare. "Get her out of here. I don't need nobody starting fights in my bar."

Roddy merely grinned at the bartender and took Lee's arm to lead her away. He never stopped smiling the whole time, until he and Lee were back out on the sidewalk. Then, he burst out laughing.

Lee appeared shocked by his behavior. "What's so

funny about what just happened?"

"You," was all he could say for several seconds. "I've been kicked out of lots of bars for starting fights, but I've never had that problem with a date."

"I guess I'm not like all the others." Her eyes were unreadable again.

"No kidding." Roddy kept laughing for several more seconds. "I'm beginning to wonder if I'm safe around you."

"I can't believe you're not mad."

"About what?"

"I ruined our night out."

"Ruined it? Honey, you *made* it. I've probably been kicked out of more bars than you've been in. Like I told you before..."

"You're not a nice boy," she finished with a wicked grin.

Roddy couldn't help it. He grabbed her and kissed her, right there in front of the Saturday night Lake Street traffic and party time revelers. He actually heard a few cheers before he finally pulled back and suggested they get a cab and find another place to go.

They asked the cab driver for a few suggestions, and Roddy picked out a couple of places they passed on the way, so they visited several more bars before they finally returned to the hotel. Since the incident in the country bar, Lee seemed more relaxed with him, more willing to let go and be her secret, uncontained self. She danced with him and for him, and wriggled her way further under his skin with every moment he spent with her.

"What do you do when you're not on tour?" she

asked him some time later when they lay sated in each other's arms. "I mean, when you're not taking road trips to visit me."

"I cause trouble, write music, and record it," he said after giving it a few seconds of thought.

"I don't even know where you live." Lee's voice sounded a little wistful.

"I have a house in Beverly Hills."

"You must think my apartment is a real dump."

"It's nicer than a hell of a lot of apartments I've lived in," he told her, trailing a fingertip over her ribs. "And yours is nice and clean. And you have books."

It was odd, Roddy mused, that he and Lee actually knew so little about each other, since it was so comfortable to be together. They had lots of innocuous questions to ask one another.

Or at least they would if they were going to have a relationship.

It felt so good, so right with her, Roddy couldn't stop his mind from wondering what was going to become of them. He wasn't ready to deal with that, though, so he pushed those thoughts away.

The following day, they spent most of their time in Roddy's hotel room, making love on the king size bed, and once, in his huge, sunken bathtub. It was Sunday, the final day of their idyll. Both were painfully aware of their limits, though they had carefully not discussed them. Obviously, Roddy had better things to do than wait around for Lee to finish work at the library every day, so he couldn't stay in Minneapolis, but Lee's life was there. There was really no place for a library clerk in his lifestyle of creating multi-million dollar recordings and going on world tours with his famous band. There was nowhere for their relationship to go, and neither wanted to face it.

They discussed everything else that came to mind, though.

"What ever made a girl like you decide to work in a stuffy old library?" Roddy wondered as they lay naked on his tangled sheets.

Lee smiled and let a hand wander freely over his skin. "I like books, and I've actually learned a lot working there. I don't have a college degree, and it's hard to find a good job without one. Plus, I'm not talented like you, and I had to work somewhere. It suits me, really."

"Very sensible. I think you're always that way."

She gave him a long, measuring look before she replied. "You'd be wrong about that."

He chuckled. "Well...maybe."

He pulled her on top of him and they came together almost desperately.

When it was over, Roddy found himself unable to keep reality at bay. He knew he should leave Minneapolis in the morning. He had a lot of things to do back in LA, and he had made only the briefest stop at his house before jumping in his car and roaring off for Minneapolis. His housekeeper probably thought he was dead. The only problem was, he didn't want to leave Lee behind. It would be impossible to go without hurting her. He wasn't such a cad he couldn't see she had feelings for him.

And since when did he care about a woman's

feelings? Quite frankly, it was something new. Just like it was unusual for him to not want to leave. Three days in any other woman's company would have sent him running for the door, and instead he found himself only reluctantly dragging his feet toward it now.

For the first time in a long time, Roddy simply did not know what to do. He decided he would figure that out in the morning when he packed Lee off to work, and for now, he would simply enjoy being with her.

He had to tear his mouth away from Lee's when the phone suddenly, loudly jangled on the bedstand. He was tempted not to answer it, but reached out to snatch the receiver nonetheless.

"What!" he barked.

He barely recognized Eddie's voice on the other end. Eddie was so drunk he could barely enunciate, but he managed to tell Roddy his tale of woe. The guitarist and his live-in girlfriend had gotten into a knock-down, drag-out fight the night before, and Eddie needed him.

"Calm down, Eddie," he cut through the slurred tirade. "I warned you about her, you know. I'll be there as soon as I can, but I'm in Minnesota with my car, so you're going to have to sit tight."

He hung up and rubbed his eyes for a moment before looking over at Lee.

She gazed back at him with huge, sad eyes, regret written all over her face.

"You have to leave." It was a statement of fact.

"I'm sorry, but I do. Eddie needs me. He's in

some seriously deep trouble right now, and he's drinking, so I have to take care of him. He's kind of like my little brother, you know?"

"You don't have to explain it to me, Roddy." Lee's voice was soft and she laid a comforting hand on his arm.

His heart swelled painfully against his ribs. Unbelievably, Lee really did seem to understand when nobody ever had before. This wasn't the first time Eddie's problems had called him away from somewhere he wanted to be, but it was the first time Roddy hadn't faced any recriminations for going to his aid. Lee did not bother to tell him Eddie was a full-grown man who could take care of himself, like Dana McMillan had once done. Lee instinctively seemed to understand everything about him in a way that no other woman ever had, or likely ever would.

So what was he supposed to do about her? He couldn't just turn his back on her and tell her it had been fun but he had to get back to his real life now. She had a life, too, and also needed to go back to hers. He couldn't ask her to return to LA with him, and quite frankly, he wasn't sure if it would be the right thing for him to do.

Lee's face was carefully blank, giving nothing away. Even her eyes were inscrutable as she gazed quietly up at him.

"Lee?" Roddy finally found his voice again. "I have to leave right away."

"I know. I can help you pack up your stuff if you want."

Her kind understanding was almost his undoing

and he looked away for a moment. "No, that's okay. I didn't bring much. I'll settle downstairs and you can stay here for awhile longer if you want."

"No." Her eyes leveled with his, and he knew she didn't want to linger alone in the room they had shared. "Don't worry about me. Just go help Eddie."

There was no anger or malice in her words, but they cut him like razors nonetheless. Suddenly, everything hurt like hell.

I am not in love with her! Roddy sternly told himself. Roddy O'Neill simply didn't fall in love.

Lee had already slid out of bed and gathered her clothes. Roddy watched silently as she slipped back into the outfit she had worn on Friday after work, but finally found his tongue when she put her shoes on and made for the door.

"Wait a minute!" he called from the bed, tossing back the sheets. "Slow down a little! I'm not in that much of a hurry. At least let me give you a ride home."

"You better not, Roddy," she said softly. He would never know if her bottom lip trembled or if it was a trick of the light.

For the second time since they'd met, the door to his hotel room closed behind her.

ଔ

"Be grateful for what you had. Be grateful for what you had," Lee murmured under her breath as she hurried down the hall away from Roddy's room. Unbidden tears coursed down her cheeks like rain.

CHAPTER EIGHT

Several times on the way home, Roddy vowed to never drive cross-country again. No matter how lead-footed he was, it still took too long and was far too agonizing when he had so many things on his mind.

On one end of the spectrum was Eddie, whose life was a real mess, thanks to gold-digging Claire. She and Eddie had been drinking too much and she started an argument with him—again. Eddie lost his temper, and in the ensuing imbroglio, Claire claimed Eddie slapped her, and she called the police. Eddie denied the charges, but had been arrested on the strength of his reputation, and now Claire was threatening to call all the tabloids—print and television—to make the story public.

Roddy knew Eddie, and Eddie did not hit women. That didn't excuse him from his participation in the mess, Roddy knew, but Eddie still did not deserve the rotten publicity Claire was about to send his way. Roddy himself had been through it, and knew it would be hell.

Hate letters from "fans" were only the tip of the iceberg. Record companies and managers didn't like that sort of publicity, no matter how many records a guy sold. Of course, Claire was fully aware of the situation. Roddy had been foolish enough to share his horror stories with her, not realizing at the time she would turn around and use the information as a weapon against Eddie.

Roddy called him often during the long drive home, but things only seemed to be getting worse on the West Coast. In addition to her battery claims, Claire was also threatening to expose Eddie as an alcoholic and drug abuser, also patently false charges.

"Okay, so I still drink a little too much sometimes, but it's not like it used to be," Eddie moaned on the phone. "I haven't done anything crazy in years!"

"I know," Roddy agreed patiently, all while his intestines tied themselves in knots. He had always been there to help Eddie out of his scrapes, and quite frankly, it was becoming tiresome. "Just try to get along with her and keep her quiet until I get there. I'll handle it as soon as I can."

"I know, Roddy," Eddie said trustingly. As usual, it was easiest for him to dump all his problems in Roddy's lap, without a thought for what Roddy might have going on himself.

Right about then, Roddy wished Lee had tried to talk some sense into him about leaving instead of being so damn understanding. In the end, Claire would accept a nice, fat payment and go her merry way, but it wouldn't happen until Eddie begged and pleaded, and Roddy resorted to threats.

At the moment, Lee not only seemed to be on the other side of the world; she might as well be on a different planet. Roddy could only smile when he thought about his Lee; sweet, soft, giving, passionate, taking, demanding Lee, who uncannily understood him like no other woman ever had. Yet he knew she wouldn't let him push her around. She would never bend over backwards or sacrifice herself for him, but he knew instinctively she would make him happy. He sensed she would fit into his life like the missing piece to a puzzle.

The only problem with Lee was that she lived half a continent away from him. He couldn't ask her to relocate to Los Angeles unless he wanted to make a pretty deep commitment, and quite honestly he wasn't ready for that. It was out of the question for him to hang out in Minneapolis for the length of time it would take for a relationship with her to fizzle. His life in California was very demanding, and wouldn't even allow him to slip away regularly on the weekends.

The only sensible thing to do about Lee was forget her. But Roddy knew he couldn't do that, no matter how hard he tried.

Every woman in tight jeans with long, blonde hair sent his heart racing until he caught a glimpse of her face. Then his heart would plummet. There was only one Lee. No one else had her soulful green eyes or her sensuous mouth that seemed to have been created solely for pleasing him. There were no other legs quite as long and shapely as hers, and the hair? Forget it. There simply wasn't hair as silky and golden as hers anywhere else in the world.

֍

Lee almost called in sick on Monday morning. She had spent a sleepless night on Sunday, thinking nonstop about Roddy. There was really no reason at all to hope that he might come back, call, or even send more flowers. That he had returned at all was a miracle unto itself. He made her no promises, though, and she wasn't foolish enough to expect any. Their time together was up, and the brief affair was over.

That she now had deep inner scars to show for it was her own fault for being stupid enough to fall in love with him. Though loath to admit it to anyone else, she knew she couldn't deny it to herself. All her efforts toward self-preservation were for naught, and her heart ran away of its own accord.

Roddy may have remembered her after their first night together, and he might even still give her a stray thought from time to time, but she suffered no illusions. He would forget about her as soon as he started another concert tour, if not before.

Seeing a smiling, curious Debbie at work was almost too much to bear. She nearly broke down and cried at the mere sight of her.

"How was your weekend?" Debbie asked in a knowing tone the moment Lee sat at her desk.

She forced a cheerful smile. "It was wonderful and you know it."

"I'll bet! I wonder what kind of flowers he'll send this time?"

"That's over, Debbie." Lee tried not to clench her teeth. "We aren't dating or anything. It was a weekend fling."

"I know that," Debbie said carefully, the first indication she knew Lee wasn't quite floating on top of the world. "But if he came all the way here, I'm sure it meant something to him."

"I'm not." Lee hated her snippy tone but couldn't control it. "He probably does stuff like that at the end of every tour."

Debbie drew in a quick breath, stunned at Lee's acerbic reaction to her attempted encouragement.

"There's probably a girl like me in every city in America," Lee went on, as much for herself as for Debbie. "Probably a few in Europe, too. I'm not going to fool myself into believing I mean anything to him."

"I will, then," Debbie said softly, her eyes filled with compassion. "Because I think you do."

The wind went out of Lee's sails and it made her sag a little, but she managed to keep her tears at bay. She hoped Debbie would start talking about something else before she disgraced herself. The last thing she wanted to think about that morning was how bleak her life suddenly seemed without Roddy in it.

As if able to sense her turmoil and needing to twist the knife, Mr. Eggers sauntered up to her desk the moment he arrived at the library.

"Miss Miller," he called out from across the room.

"Yes, Mr. Eggers?" Her answer contained all the enthusiasm of a condemned man on his way to the executioner. He was sure to reprimand her about bringing her social life into the library, and then give her a nice, long speech about the gross impropriety of it.

Eggers looked thoughtful when he stopped in front of her desk. "That gentleman you left with on Friday," he said, his tone conspicuous for the lack of condemnation within. "I thought I recognized him from somewhere."

"Probably." Her voice was noncommittal.

"Is he from around here? I don't believe I've ever seen him in the library before, and I can't quite place him."

Lee had to wonder if he was asking her about Roddy just to be malicious. Surely he had to know talking about Roddy so soon after his departure was painful.

"I don't think he's been in before," she said casually. "He lives in California."

Eggers's eyebrows shot up above his glasses. "California! What on earth was he doing here?"

Lee felt like screaming at him to mind his own business, but it would be fruitless, as well as unwise. She needed her job, and he wouldn't leave her alone until she told him what he wanted to know. Still, she wasn't going to just hand over the information; Eggers would have to work for it.

She gave him a slight smile. "He came here to visit me, Mr. Eggers." Lee was proud of her even tone, though she narrowed her eyes just slightly.

His widened. "Really. How do you come to know a gentleman like...you never did mention his name."

"No, I didn't."

Eggers smiled. "Well? How did you meet such a man?" He was apparently willing to be just as persistent as she was determined to be evasive.

"At a concert."

His tight-lipped mouth pursed itself into an O. "A concert! How fascinating. I have a feeling it wasn't the philharmonic."

She smiled back now but her tone was clipped. "Excellent guess."

Eggers scowled and pursed his lips again. He waited a beat for more information, and then finally asked, "Well, who is he?"

"He's Roddy O'Neill," was Lee's flat reply. Her smile vanished and her eyes dropped down to stare at her desk.

Oblivious to her distress, Eggers repeated the name. "Roddy O'Neill. You know, the name really is familiar, but I still can't place it."

"*This* Roddy O'Neill!" Debbie almost shouted, shocking Lee out of her momentary lethargy. Up until that moment, Debbie had quietly seethed behind her desk while she glared holes into Mr. Eggers's back. When he turned to gape at her, she almost viciously flung a glossy magazine at him.

Eggers caught it neatly and his eyes lit up. "Ah, yes. Of course. The infamous Roddy O'Neill, the rock star. How interesting that he came here to see you, Lee. I suppose he was also the romantic fool sending all the flowers."

Debbie's outburst had shocked some life back into Lee, and she responded with some of her usual fire. "Yes, I guess he's that same romantic fool."

Eggers raised a supercilious brow. "I don't see any flowers today." His tone was almost conversational.

"I knew they upset you, so I asked him not to send any more," Lee lied. She certainly didn't want to hear his opinions on the state of her affair with Roddy if he found out no more flowers or anything else would be forthcoming.

"That was a wise decision." Eggers's voice was flat. "I don't suppose I'll have to worry about him or anyone of his ilk wandering into the library again." He looked at his fingernails. "I expect you to make up the time you missed on Friday afternoon. I have some things to do at another branch today, so I'm afraid you girls will have to do without my supervision. I trust you will accomplish a few things in my absence."

"Of course," Lee said with a tight smile, noting Debbie just fixed him with a noncommittal stare.

Lee threw a box of pencils at the door when it closed behind him.

"Forget him, Lee," Debbie admonished softly. "He's just upset because you fell short of his high expectations."

"Ha!" Lee snorted. "What expectations are those?"

"Library clerks aren't supposed to have sex, you know. And if they do, certainly not with long-haired, tattooed rock and rollers!"

Lee had to laugh at that, and for the moment at least, her spirits lifted. Debbie was right. Though he was strict and overly stuffy, Mr. Eggers usually had a soft spot for her. He actually looked upon himself as some sort of surrogate parent for Lee, since he was aware of her strained relationship with her family. His unusual interest in Roddy, and his acidic reaction to him, were just his way of showing his disapproval of her choice in men without coming right out and telling Lee how he felt.

As the week wore on and Mr. Eggers seemed to start forgiving her, Lee's life became a little more bearable. She tried not to let it depress her that Roddy sent no more flowers. It was time to let go of her foolish dreams about him anyway. She could afford no illusions about Roddy O'Neill. They had had fun together, and that was that. He probably had at least a million fans in love with him who would never even get to experience that much, and she should be glad she got to know him at all.

Still, no matter what she told herself, there was an ache inside that felt as if it would never heal. It was hard to believe their encounters had meant absolutely nothing to Roddy when she remembered the way he had treated her so tenderly. After all, he hadn't been able to forget about her after their first night together. Then, he spent a small fortune on flowers for her, and to cap it off, he drove across the country to see her at his first opportunity. It was hard to write it all off as a meaningless fling in light of all that.

Lee knew, though, that if she really meant something to him, he would not completely disappear from her life. She managed to dredge up excuses for him anyhow. Roddy didn't send more flowers or call because Eddie was in deep trouble, and he was busy night and day helping him out. Or, Roddy couldn't call because he was too busy in the studio working on new recordings. The excuse she refused to even entertain was that Roddy didn't call her because he was just as blown away by the chemistry between them as she was, and didn't know how to work her into his busy life.

Lee threw herself into her job, working harder and more diligently than ever before. Mr. Eggers was exceedingly pleased. He beamed when she finished two large projects well under the deadline and then offered to work late to help him catch up on some past-due assignments and other assorted tasks. She was finally back in his good graces, it seemed.

"I saw an article about your rock star friend," he said conversationally one evening when they were the only ones in the library. He tossed her a magazine he normally wouldn't have given a glance.

Lee caught it and spied Roddy on the cover, singing his heart out to a crowd of thousands while sweat poured off his face. The story inside appeared to be a generic piece about the band's concert tour with a fabricated paragraph about Roddy and Dana McMillan's hot affair.

Lee was tempted to tell Mr. Eggers that Dana McMillan meant nothing to Roddy and that the article was all lies, but she didn't want to admit to herself or anyone else that she was jealous of the other woman, even though Roddy insisted she was part of his past. She realized Eggers probably tossed her the magazine just because of the nugget about Dana, and she was determined not to react to it.

She set the magazine aside. "I think I've read that article already," she murmured. "It seems outdated, since the tour ended a few weeks ago. Those kind of magazines are such tripe. They should hire some decent reporters so they'd be worth reading."

"Nobody really wants to hear the truth," Eggers commented in a casual tone of voice, though his message came across loud and clear.

Lee gave him a serene smile. "I think I'm wise enough to separate fact from fiction," she said quietly before turning her attention to the papers on her desk. She wished Mr. Eggers would just leave her alone about Roddy. The last thing she needed right then was someone dredging up things she didn't want to think about.

"I've always thought you had a level head." Mr. Eggers gave her a fatherly smile.

A compliment from him was rare, and Lee recognized it as more of a warning.

"I like to think so," she told him as she rose from her chair. She made an excuse about needing to find a book so she could leave the room and end the tedious conversation.

ଔ

Life in Minneapolis was a veritable haven in comparison to Roddy's existence in Los Angeles. From the moment he drove over the California border, he forced himself to put Lee out of his mind, at least for awhile.

He drove straight to Eddie's house in the Hollywood hills, and walked in without knocking. Claire had the nerve to still be there, draped uselessly over a couch, and she glared hatefully at him as he strode past her without so much as a hello. Roddy made his way back to the study where, as expected, Eddie was nursing a huge bottle of whiskey, despite his promises not to drink until Roddy arrived.

"Roddy!" he cried, lurching out of his chair to enfold his best friend in a bear hug. "I knew I could count on you. I'm glad you're finally here."

"What is Claire doing here?" Roddy asked without preamble.

"Whoa, calm down, man," Eddie slurred, backing up and falling into a chair. "I had to keep her quiet somehow until you got here, so I told her she could stay."

"I thought I told you to stay sober." Roddy glared at Eddie, hating that he had to assume the big brother role yet again. He knew from experience that nothing else would work when his friend had been drinking, though.

"Shyeah, easier said than done with Claire in the house." Eddie laughed grimly and then sloshed more whiskey down his throat.

"Have you at least talked to your lawyer?"

Eddie wiped his mouth with the back of his hand. "Yeah, I'm not completely stupid. He told me I should pay her off if that's what it takes to shut her up and get her out of here."

Roddy snatched the whiskey bottle before Eddie could hit it again and slammed it decisively on a table.

"I'll do what I can to help out," he said with a stern glare. "But you need to make me a promise, and keep it this time. Sober up, and don't drink another drop until I get Claire to sign something and get her out of here. That means all her stuff, too. I want her gone for good this time."

"Yes, Mommy."

Roddy whirled on him, thrusting his scowling face just inches from Eddie's. "If you don't want my help…"

Eddie deflated and looked at the floor. "Okay, okay. Sorry."

"Claire!" Roddy suddenly thundered, causing Eddie to moan and cover his ears while he sank into a chair again.

She appeared in the doorway almost instantly. Roddy noted that as usual, her hair looked perfect, and why wouldn't it? A woman like Claire had absolutely nothing to do with her time but perfect her appearance. Her bottle-blonde mane and traffic-stopping body were stuffed into a short miniskirt and a halter top, and she looked ready to pose for absent paparazzi. He supposed he might have found her beautiful if not for her self-serving, greedy nature and the petulance marring her features.

"What do you want?" she asked coldly from the doorway.

"I think it's more like, what do you want?" Roddy stared her down.

Spots of color appeared in her cheeks as she worked herself into a snit. Red-tipped fingers clenched in fists at her sides, and she stepped angrily into the room.

"Did he tell you that he *hit* me?" she screeched.

Roddy gave her an infuriating smile. "I heard his side of things, yes. So what do you want?"

"An apology, for starters."

Roddy's smile disappeared. "Perhaps I should rephrase my question. *How much* do you want?"

"I don't think money can compensate for the hell he's put me through!" Claire whined, her lower lip stuck out in a girlish pout.

At that moment, an image of Lee flashed through Roddy's mind. He knew Lee would never act like this. She would never be with a man for his money and fame, he was sure. Lee would also never dye her hair such an obvious color, paint her clothes on, or wear that much make-up before the sun went down.

Roddy clenched his teeth. Why was he doomed to compare every damn woman he saw to Lee?

He turned his frustration on Claire. "Cut the crap," he snapped, startling her somewhat. He knew she needed to be treated with an iron fist in a kid glove, but he was just plain tired of her and everything she stood for. "Most women I know wouldn't call your life in Hollywood, or shopping on Rodeo Drive, hell."

Claire tossed her head. "What about his sleeping around? Putting up with that is hell."

Leave it to Claire to suddenly care about that.

"I don't see a ring on your finger," Roddy reminded her, deliberately bringing up a sore point. Claire had been unsuccessful in her attempts to get her hands permanently on Eddie's money.

"I never asked her to marry me!" Eddie chose that moment to interject. He earned two icy glares for the effort.

"A man shouldn't have to be married not to screw around," Claire complained.

"Maybe not," Roddy agreed, thinking that if Lee lived with him, he wouldn't have the desire for another woman, much less the energy. "But I don't think you were ever under any illusions."

Claire got a stubborn set to her jaw. "I want more from him."

"Name your price." Roddy's tone was exasperated.

She still felt the need to keep up a façade. "I'm not some hooker!" she shrilled.

"Of course not." Roddy quietly disagreed. Despite the situation, though, he would not voice his opinion in front of Eddie. He didn't give a damn about Claire. He sighed and forced himself to sound calm and reasonable while he lied through his teeth. "It's obvious you and Eddie cared for each other a lot at one time, but things just aren't working out anymore. I'm sure Eddie's sorry about your fight and everything that happened. I know he didn't mean to hurt you, but maybe you've hurt him a little, too."

"Hurt that reptile?" Claire huffed.

Roddy's eyes got steely. "I'm prepared to take Eddie on every talk show in the country with two beautiful girls who will go on and on about how sweet he is. You know that's gonna shoot all kinds of holes through your story about abuse, and it'll make you look like nothing more than a gold-digging bitch who couldn't get her claws in deep enough to get a ring on her finger before he tossed you out."

Claire got quiet all of a sudden. Roddy knew she enjoyed her status in Hollywood as the live-in girlfriend of a famous rock star. Her image would be irreparably tarnished if Eddie went on TV and badmouthed her to the world. She would be a laughingstock. With her limited talents, it would seriously hamper her chances of hooking up with another guy of Eddie's stature.

Roddy watched her calculating her options before she turned to him and said, "I've been living here for two years."

"I'm sure Eddie is willing to compensate you for all the effort you've made toward the upkeep of his house, and for making him so deliriously happy all that time," Roddy forced himself to say. It was hard to do without curling his lip.

"Fifty thousand," Eddie suddenly said decisively from his slumped position in the chair.

Claire's lips thinned for a moment, but then she nodded. "Okay."

Roddy felt in that moment he could almost read her mind. He knew she hated him for stepping in and ruining her plans. Though their relationship had been rocky, Claire would have a hard time finding another man like Eddie. Roddy knew her original intent had been to get Eddie to hand her a large sum of money, and then to stick around to keep milking him for more. Of course, Roddy had ruined that for her and now she was on her way out of his life for good.

"She better not come back," Roddy warned Eddie once she left the room. He couldn't explain why she had been allowed to stay as long as she had. "If you let her back in here, I'm not going to help you out again."

CALIFORNIA DREAM

Eddie laughed, already forgetting his problems now that Roddy was making them go away. "I must've interrupted something good!"

Roddy met his careless comment with a glower. "We aren't going to talk about my love life today."

Eddie ignored the warning. "So now it's love life instead of sex life, huh? I knew it. I knew the minute you started writing that damn song you'd lost it. It had to happen sooner or later."

"Just like you and Claire?"

Eddie gave him a cocky look. "Hey, we both know what Claire always was to me."

"Not really," Roddy murmured.

"Bummer she lives so far away." Eddie changed the subject back to Lee as if Roddy had not spoken. "What are you going to do about that?

"Nothing."

"Yet. You're going to get tired of traveling to Minneapolis all the time."

"I'm not going back to Minneapolis."

"Sending somebody a one-way ticket to LA?"

"No!"

"Then you're going back to Minneapolis." Eddie was really starting to wear on Roddy's nerves.

"Says who?"

"Says five hundred bucks."

Roddy glared balefully at his best friend. "I guess I could use another pair of boots."

Eddie grinned back. "I can always use some new toys."

Roddy noticed his friend no longer seemed so helpless, or drunk. Instead, he seemed to be having fun playing devil's advocate. He was forcing Roddy to think about things he wanted to push out of his mind at the moment. And, he was planting ideas in Roddy's head that he shouldn't entertain.

Sending Lee a ticket to LA was a crazy idea. She had a job and friends and a life in Minneapolis and wouldn't be willing to leave it all behind. Still, Roddy couldn't quiet the little voice in his head that kept asking why, if her life there was so fulfilling, she had dropped everything and thrown herself into a weekend affair with him without having to make even a single phone call.

He left Eddie's house in a pensive mood, damning his friend for planting seeds in his head. Just like that, his mind was working on solutions to problems that had seemed insurmountable only a couple of days ago.

Before he could effect any changes in his life, though, he did have one person he needed to see. It had been ages since Roddy paid a visit to his mother.

Margaret O'Neill lived in a modest house in Pasadena. Roddy had wanted to buy her something much grander, but she insisted on staying in her small, two-bedroom dwelling in its quiet, unassuming neighborhood.

Some days, Roddy was glad she had insisted. Every time he went to visit her, it brought him back down to earth, which he especially needed after the hype and glitz of a concert tour. Sometimes he needed the reminder that underneath it all, he was just an average guy who happened to have a lucrative career. He didn't want to start believing his own press, which was easy to do when he retired to a beautiful home in Beverly Hills at the end of the day.

Roddy's mother was having coffee with a neighbor when his Maserati pulled into her driveway. He noticed her through her kitchen window when he hopped out of the car and loped up the front walk. She met him at the door, and he enveloped her in a bear hug, then twirled her around in circles.

Her neighbor said a smiling hello, then excused herself, knowing Roddy hadn't been to see his mother in months. Roddy knew she would get all the details of his visit later on.

Margaret laughed and demanded Roddy set her down before her neighbor had closed the door. "Even after all those girls on tour, you've still got so much energy!" she remarked.

"There weren't that many," he argued, giving her a squeeze.

"At least not on the second half, hmm?" Margaret asked wisely.

Roddy ignored the comment. "How are you, Ma?"

"I'm fine, dear. But I have to admit I've been a little worried about you. Eddie told me you had to take care of some kind of business in Minneapolis."

Roddy scowled. "When did you talk to Eddie?"

Margaret made a face and waved her hands. "When that Claire was making her threats. You weren't here, so he called to ask me for advice."

"I can't believe he dragged you into his problems," he grumbled.

"It's okay, Roddy," she said gently. "Eddie needs

a mother, since he hasn't spoken to his own parents in over ten years. By the way, how is he?"

Roddy sighed long and hard. "He's okay now. He paid Claire off and I dropped her at a friend's house to make sure she really left."

"I can't figure out why he ever let her move in."

"You're not alone," Roddy mused. "He seems to like having someone around. Maybe it gives him some sort of security to keep someone soft and warm at home, no matter how far he travels."

Margaret nodded wisely. "I'm just glad she's gone. I never liked that woman." She paused a beat, and then fixed her son with a look. "I'm sure that girl in Minneapolis would never behave like her."

Roddy turned away and said nothing for several seconds, then slowly turned to regard his mother through narrowed eyes. "Probably not."

Margaret just stared back at him for several seconds before she finally said, "What are you going to do about her, Roddy?"

"How do you even know about her, Ma?"

She gave him a long, hard stare that told him he couldn't hide anything from her. "Eddie told me, of course. He seems quite happy for you, too, since I convinced him you will still be able to function, even if you are in love."

"Ma! For God's sake! Why does everyone keep saying that?" Roddy ran his hands through his hair.

"Because you drove halfway across the country just to see her, that's why," was Margaret's calm answer. "And Roddy O'Neill hasn't crossed the street for a woman since he got rich and famous."

"So?"

Margaret was not deterred by his attitude. "Are you going to marry her, Roddy?"

He thought his eyes would pop right out of their sockets. "I guess I haven't thought that far ahead, since I barely even know her!"

"That doesn't really matter."

"Maybe not for a normal guy, but everything I do winds up on the front page of a magazine. I have to be careful."

"Ha! If anyone can afford to live a little, it's you. Didn't I read a quote from you somewhere that bragged you do whatever you want?"

"I don't do marriage."

"So you're going to keep chasing everything in a skirt until you're too old to walk?" Margaret's tone was caustic. "That sounds pretty stupid, if you ask me."

Very patiently, and very slowly, Roddy attempted to explain. "Guys like me don't have to get married."

Margaret rolled her eyes. "You're right, Roddy. Just play around until you're tired, and then settle for someone like Claire. That's a great idea."

"What's gotten into you?" Roddy tried hard not to shout, but failed.

His mother was undeterred. "Eddie says she's a librarian, and smart. Not like all those stupid girls I've had to put up with over the years. You don't think a woman like that is going to settle for half of a relationship, do you?"

"For the last time, there is no relationship, and there never will be!" Roddy's voice shook the windows.

"You'll never get her to give up her job and family unless you've got something to offer," Margaret said calmly.

Roddy knew she was still smiling when he slammed out of her house.

CHAPTER NINE

Roddy was most irritated with his mother because she knew him too well. He could only hope she had not also discerned Lee's character as accurately as she thought because no matter what he did, he could not get Lee off his mind.

It was an impossible situation. Lee lived in Minneapolis, while Roddy's life was in Los Angeles. Roddy had obligations and a multi-million dollar career in Los Angeles. There was simply no way he could leave it all behind and run off to Minneapolis. The idea was ludicrous. But it seemed equally ludicrous to ask Lee to give up her job and friends to move to Los Angeles, didn't it? It wasn't as if Roddy was prepared to ask her to marry him. Realistically, he knew he wouldn't even have all that much time to spend with her if she lived in LA. He could only imagine her reaction if he asked her to give up her job and leave the life she knew behind so he could fit her into his busy schedule on the West Coast.

So he was back where he started, and the only sensible thing to do about Lee was nothing. He would just have to forget her. That doing it was impossible was something he would have to learn to live with. It was his fault he had been foolish enough to let her tangle in his emotions, and now he would have to suffer the consequences.

Eddie saw things from a different perspective. For some ridiculous reason, he blamed Lee for Roddy's inability to devote the necessary efforts to their music. Roddy's inattention affected the whole band, not just Roddy himself, and Eddie had fun reminding his best friend of his obligations every time they saw each other.

"That piece really sucks, Rod," Eddie said point-blank one day at the end of rehearsal.

When Roddy would have gone off, Zeke tactfully piped up, "I think he means it's not as good as your usual stuff."

"No, I meant it sucks," Eddie insisted. "Maybe we can sell it to a teenybopper bubble-gum band, but it's not going on a record with my name."

"He's got a point," Mike quietly agreed. "Any song you write can be sold."

"But nobody wants to do that one," Roddy grumbled.

There were nods and murmurs of assent all around.

"Anyone got any better ideas?" he asked, glowering at the band.

"What about that song you were working on during the tour?" David suggested as he carefully set his guitar on the floor.

Eddie cracked a grin, but kept his mouth shut for once.

Roddy stopped short. "I don't want to do that

CALIFORNIA DREAM

one."

"But it's great!" Mike chimed in from his quiet corner. "I mean, that song is inspired! The lyrics rock, and Eddie's guitar part is sheer dynamite. That song is a hit waiting to happen."

"I said I don't want to do that one." Roddy's tone got cold and deadly.

Generally, when Roddy took that tone of voice, the other guys backed off, but Eddie just grinned.

"Roddy's a little…ah…sentimental about that song, guys," he said on a chuckle.

"What?" Zeke snorted. "Rod's the guy who always told us sentiment sells."

"It's not exactly the song he's sentimental about," Eddie found it necessary to explain.

"Shut up, Eddie." Roddy's voice was glacial.

Eddie and Roddy went way back, and were as close as brothers. The other guys wouldn't push their leader if he got stubborn, but Eddie wouldn't allow that to stop him. If he believed the song would be a hit, he would put the best interests of all of them first, not just Roddy's emotions. Instead of showing any remorse for his behavior, Eddie just sat there and grinned.

Bolstered by his offhand attitude, the other guys decided to ignore Roddy's bad mood and sided with Eddie.

"So you wrote a song about a girl. So what? It's not the first time that's ever happened," Mike piped up.

Before Roddy could put him off, Eddie chimed in. "Mike, it's the first time *Roddy* has ever felt this way about a girl and wrote a song about it."

A chorus of, "Oh," went through their ranks.

"Roddy's in love!" Zeke couldn't resist chanting.

Roddy glared balefully at all of them. "You're acting like a bunch of high school kids," he snapped. "Just because I don't want to capitalize on this one song…"

"Our contracts say we get to vote on the songs he writes," Eddie interrupted his excuses. "And since I co-wrote this one, I can automatically put it up for the vote. So, who wants to record *I Could Love Her?*"

Everyone but Roddy voted for the song.

"And who wants to be associated with this piece of trash?" Eddie asked, waving a sheaf of papers in the air.

Not even Roddy voted for it, which said volumes to the band. It wasn't like him to give in so easily.

ଔ

Lee and Debbie shared a pizza in the middle of Lee's tiny living room. Debbie was engaged in a show Lee didn't enjoy while Lee scowled over her bills.

"Now I know why some girls get married right out of high school," she grumbled. "It would be so nice to lay all this responsibility on someone else's shoulders for once."

"And when you got home from a long day of work for slave wages, you could cook his dinner and pick up after him, too," Debbie said on a laugh.

Lee crinkled her nose in distaste. "Aren't there any other options?"

"Sure. Find someone rich so he'll hire someone

else to cook and clean," was Debbie's flip reply.

Lee turned wistful. "I bet he has a maid."

There was no need to clarify who "he" was. There was only one man on Lee's mind of late, and that was Roddy O'Neill.

"Why don't you call him and ask?"

Debbie offered the suggestion lightly, but Lee did not smile. It was hard to gauge her reaction to anything, since lately she was either depressed, on edge, or simply off in another world where no one else was allowed to go.

"He forgot to give me his number," she said absently.

Even if she had a phone number for Roddy, she knew she wouldn't call him. She would never go chasing after a man who was no longer interested in her, even if he was all she could think about. Lee knew Debbie was irked that Roddy hadn't given her any contact information, though she didn't say anything about it. No doubt, Debbie knew Lee would just defend Roddy's actions or lack thereof, and neither of them wanted to have that conversation.

"Maybe he'll call you, and then you can ask him all sorts of questions," Debbie said gently. She tried to sound casual, but Lee could see through it.

"He's not going to call." There was finality in Lee's tone. "If he was going to call, he would have done it by now. He's been gone for six weeks."

"But he drove all the way here to see you," Debbie insisted, her words laced with exasperation. "If he went to the trouble, don't you think he'll at least call?"

"No."

Lee could see her calm assurance drove Debbie up the wall.

Debbie tossed the remote onto the couch in irritation. "So, that's it, huh? You've never been the kind of person to stand still for being used, Lee. So why this time? Is it because he's famous and all that? I thought that kind of thing didn't make a difference to you."

"Damn it, Debbie, it doesn't!" Lee shouted. "And he didn't use me any more than I used him, okay? It's just over between us because we live a thousand miles apart."

"I'm sorry, Lee." Debbie was immediately contrite.

Lee didn't like to dwell on heartbreak, especially since love seemed to elude her in all aspects of life. She wasn't one to sit around and cry because her mother abandoned her when she was young and her father took his anger and frustration out on her. She didn't whine because they lived in the same city but he never called unless he wanted something. Instead, she tried to harden herself to life's disappointments.

She knew Debbie could sense the strain. Lee and Debbie were as close as sisters, and Debbie sometimes looked up to her as if she was older and wiser. Lee knew Debbie wouldn't antagonize her or cause her sadness for anything in the world, and that she was very bothered by Lee's behavior since Roddy O'Neill had come and gone.

Debbie was probably thinking the last thing Lee needed was someone like Roddy. Men like him used women and cast them aside without a thought. Someday, Lee wanted to meet someone who would love and cherish her, and offer her the moon. She knew that man wasn't Roddy O'Neill, and he wasn't going to offer her anything, so it was best to move on.

She was annoyed with herself for walking into the situation with her eyes wide open. She had not asked Roddy for anything because she didn't expect anything from him. So why was she still clinging to a tiny kernel of hope? Why had she allowed herself to fall for him? Why not someone like Paul, who was stable. Paul was sweet and kind, and a life with someone like him would not be fraught with insecurity. Loving someone like him seemed as if it would be so natural and easy, but Lee's heart apparently wasn't interested in that.

The truth of the matter was that falling for Roddy was the most natural thing in the world. Roddy was nothing like Paul. He was wild and daring, while Paul was staid and conservative. Roddy's attraction to her had been about nothing but herself. He noticed and appreciated her individuality, like her long, unruly hair and the bright colors she liked to wear. Those were two things Paul had not really seemed to appreciate. Roddy had taken her out to parts of town Paul wouldn't visit, and Lee had loved every minute of it. Even being thrown out of the bar on Lake Street had been an adventure. How could she not love a man who seemed happy with her just the way she was?

She turned to confront Debbie's concerned gaze. "I'm sorry," she said as evenly as she could. "I guess

I'm just a little touchy about Roddy. Just because he won't be calling me again doesn't make him a bad guy. A relationship between us is just impossible."

☙

Roddy and Eddie sprawled in chairs out by Roddy's pool. The moon shone a silver stripe on the black water, and the only other light came from the glowing red ends of two cigarettes.

Roddy's red glow bobbed up and down in agitation as he emphasized a point. "It has nothing to do with her!"

"Bull," Eddie said plainly. "Since you came back from Minneapolis, you've been worthless. You moon around like a lovesick calf."

"I do not."

Eddie's teeth gleamed in the moonlight when he laughed. "You haven't churned out a decent song since you came back."

"I do not *churn out* music," Roddy hissed through clenched teeth.

"Not lately," Eddie agreed, undeterred by Roddy's rising temper. "But I've got an idea."

"This should be good." Roddy snorted.

"What do you say to giving this girl of yours a vacation?"

"What?"

"Calm down," Eddie soothed. "No strings attached for you, of course, and you'll be honest with her, so she can't accuse you of stringing her along and breaking her heart."

Roddy fixed him with a look. "Go on."

"Invite her to come here for a visit. Set her up in a

nice little suite at the Beverly Hills and keep her there until you're over her. A week or two should do the trick. She ought to be thrilled. Find me a girl who doesn't want a posh vacation in one of the finest hotels in California."

Roddy, who had always been extremely casual about matters concerning the opposite sex, very nearly vaulted out of his chair to knock Eddie and his smug smile into the pool. The nerve of the man to suggest Lee be treated like a piece of baggage and sent on her way once he was through with her!

Still, something in Eddie's suggestion struck him as a good idea.

Why not invite Lee to California for a vacation? Surely even librarians were given time off every now and then, weren't they? It wouldn't be outrageous to invite Lee to visit for a couple of weeks, and couldn't necessarily be construed as leading her on. He also wouldn't be committing himself to anything he wasn't ready for. The idea seemed perfect.

Aloud, he told Eddie, "That's the stupidest idea I've ever heard."

"Why?" he asked with a raised brow. "I think it's perfect. Foolproof, actually. It's…"

"I'm not setting her up in some hotel when I've got at least five extra bedrooms here. I don't want to have to drive across town every day. She'll stay with me."

The wattage in Eddie's grin rivaled Las Vegas. "Call her now."

"It's after eleven o'clock."

"In California. In Minnesota, it's only nine."

Roddy thought about it for a moment, and then smiled. Why not?

It was ridiculous that he actually felt nervous about calling Lee. He hadn't felt that way about a girl since he was a teenager. Roddy O'Neill wasn't supposed to be nervous about anything but record sales.

He glared at his grinning best friend as he reached for the telephone. "Why don't you go empty the rest of my refrigerator?"

"I'm not hungry."

"Then go make yourself a drink." Roddy's tone brooked no argument, so with another infuriating grin, Eddie lumbered off into the house.

Quashing his trepidation, Roddy picked up the phone and dialed the number he had never called that was still burned into his memory. Disappointingly, the phone rang several times and he was just about to disconnect when it was finally picked up.

Lee's growly voice was decidedly unfriendly. "Who the hell is this, and why are you calling me at one o'clock in the morning?"

Roddy scowled and vowed to skin Eddie alive. Leave it to his best friend to do the math backwards and make him look like a jerk.

"Lee?" he said uncertainly. He hoped she wouldn't just hang up or tell him to kiss off and never call again. He refused to analyze why he was suddenly so nervous about it.

His fears flew away on wings when her tone immediately softened. "Roddy?"

"Yeah. I guess you remember me." His heart lifted immeasurably.

"I told you I would." Lee's voice was a couple octaves lower than what Roddy was used to. "I can't believe you actually remembered me."

"I have so got to work on my image," he muttered.

"Calling and waking me up on a work night isn't going to help you."

"I'm sorry." Roddy was immediately contrite. "I got the time difference mixed up."

"I think I can forgive you, just this once."

Roddy was unaccountably happy just hearing her voice. Everything about her was so much different than any other woman in his experience. Anyone else would have forgiven him immediately for his transgression, simply because he was a rock star. Lee treated him like he was a regular guy who had to play by the rules. He knew he couldn't get away with whatever he wanted with Lee, and he found he liked it. Instead of being annoyed, he respected her. He hadn't been able to respect a woman in that way in a long, long time.

"Maybe you'd feel more forgiving if you got to take a nice vacation," he suggested.

"What kind of vacation?"

He could tell immediately she was suspicious, and the memory of her shoving his money back into his pocket came to mind.

"I was hoping you'd want to come and see the sights in California," he said quickly.

Lee sighed. "I'd love to, but I can't."

Roddy's heart sank. "Why not?"

"I'm still saving for a car, so I can't drive out there,

and if I had the money for plane fare, I'd already be somewhere fun." Roddy could tell she hated to admit to limited finances, and it gave him another ridiculous rush.

"Don't worry about it. I've got it," he interjected before she could give him another reason. When she started in with the expected objections, he cut her off. "Don't give me your kept woman line. I need you out here for selfish reasons."

There was a moment of silence before she said, "Oh? What kind of selfish reasons?"

He chuckled and ran a hand through his hair. "The band is going to lynch me if I don't get back to work pretty soon. I've been pretty worthless for the last few weeks, and Eddie has them convinced it's your fault."

"Oh, please."

"I mean it! They don't like any of the new songs I've given them, and they think my mind is somewhere else."

"That's just crazy."

"No kidding," Roddy agreed, a fraction too emphatically. "The bottom line is, unless I can get you to agree to come out and visit me for a couple of weeks, my four best friends are going to seek other employment."

He waited while Lee mulled over his suggestion. He hoped she would forget her scruples and just accept the invitation. He knew she was independent and self-supporting, but he hoped she would swallow her pride and let him pay for her tickets just this once. It was the only way they would get to see each other.

It felt like several minutes had passed when he finally heard Lee sigh.

"I can't be held responsible for the break-up of an American legend," she said carefully. "I guess I have to come."

Roddy's heart soared, and he clenched his phone a little tighter. "When?"

She sighed again. "I have to arrange for time off work," she explained. "I'll have to let you know."

"How soon?"

Roddy could picture her smile. "I go in tomorrow at eight o'clock, and I'll ask Eggers for the time off as soon as I get there. I can tell you tomorrow."

"Call me as soon as you find out."

"It'll be just after six a.m. in California."

"I don't care. Just call me right away."

"Um…Roddy?"

"Yeah."

"I can't call you."

"Why not?"

"Your number was blocked on my caller ID."

Roddy slapped his forehead at his stupidity. All this time, he had been so busy sorting out his feelings, he hadn't even thought about Lee not being able to contact him. No wonder she always expected the worst. He quickly rattled off his number.

"I guess I'll call you at an indecent hour of morning, then," Lee promised in a husky voice.

Roddy was reluctant to let her off the phone now that he had her on the line, but he remembered that she had to go to work the next day. Reluctantly, he rang off, and told himself it was enough he had already interrupted her sleep. There was no need to keep her up all night, too.

ಊ

Lee found it impossible to get back to sleep after Roddy called. How was a woman supposed to sleep when she had the prospect of a vacation in California to look forward to? The vacation itself was exciting, but her feelings went off the charts since she would be spending it with Roddy O'Neill. The whole thing sounded like a game show prize, and she was having a hard time believing it was her real life.

She knew she looked like hell the following morning when she stumbled into work. After wrestling with it twice as long as usual, she simply accepted she was having a bad hair day. No amount of make-up could hide the dark circles under her eyes. She dressed in a flattering color, but it apparently didn't help.

"Late night last night?" Eggers snapped at her when she dragged herself to her desk.

She gave him a sheepish smile. "I had trouble sleeping."

"I see."

Lee decided to ignore the butterflies going crazy in her stomach and get business out of the way immediately. She straightened in her chair and gave her boss a serious look.

"I have two weeks of vacation in the bank, don't I?" she asked

He checked the book he always kept handy at his desk. "More, actually."

"I'd like to take some time off."

Mr. Eggers looked at her sharply. While he seemed to enjoy riding herd on her and Debbie, Lee knew he thought she was a good worker. Their professional relationship felt a little strained for awhile after Roddy showed up at the library, but Lee's diligence got her back in his good graces. Lee couldn't think of a reason for Mr. Eggers to deny her request. She had not taken a substantial amount of time off in well over year. She was sure her boss would not approve of the way she wanted to use her vacation days, but it really was none of his business.

"How soon would you like to go?" Mr. Eggers asked in a careful tone. Maybe he had already guessed she would take the time off whether he liked it or not.

She smiled and shrugged. "As soon as you can spare me, I guess."

He was definitely displeased, but surprisingly, gave in immediately. "If you need time off, I think I can let you go by Monday. Just finish out the week, and then I guess we'll find a way to manage without you."

A slow smile spread over Lee's features. "Thank you, Mr. Eggers. I also need to make a long-distance phone call. Do you have one of those slips for me to fill out?"

He looked like he wanted to grill her about the necessity of the call, but he merely thinned his lips and reached into a drawer. He wordlessly handed her a slip and then discreetly left the room so she could make her call in private, though he shook his head and muttered on the way out.

Lee counted to three after the door shut at his back, and then immediately began dialing.

Roddy's phone rang several times, and she was scared she had the wrong number until finally, his familiar, gravelly voice answered.

"H'lo." It was obvious Roddy had been awakened from a deep sleep.

"I can't believe you weren't waiting up all night for my call," Lee teased in a flippant tone.

Roddy's response was a deep, raspy chuckle. He obviously recognized her voice, and it made Lee feel tingly all over.

"I was waiting by the phone," he told her, "but I guess I fell asleep." There was a pause while he made a few rustling sounds. "I'm wearing yesterday's clothes and I still have my boots on."

"I'm just calling to see if your invitation is still open," Lee said through the smile that wouldn't leave her lips.

"Of course it is." His voice was light, but held an undertone of seriousness.

"Good. I wanted to let you know I can come out any time after five o'clock on Friday."

Roddy was quiet for a few seconds, and Lee's heart hammered away as she feared he would tell her he had changed his mind.

Instead, he murmured, "Mmm. I guess I can wait 'til Friday night. I'll get you the first possible flight."

Since she was at work, they kept their conversation short, and Lee hung up the phone feeling dazed. It seemed too good to be true, but she was leaving to visit Roddy before the week was out.

She attacked her work with vigor all week to keep herself from dwelling on the upcoming vacation. She had to make sure she was exhausted at the end of the day or sleep would have been impossible. Every day after work, she went shopping for the things she was certain she would need. It was only a two-week vacation, but Lee had a feeling her life was undergoing irrevocable changes.

Lee had Roddy's number now, and was tempted every day to use it, but she held herself back. She didn't want him to get sick of her before she even arrived. She hoped he might call again, but he was obviously busy because he did not. Her ticket arrived in her e-mail right on schedule, though.

On Friday, Debbie borrowed a car from a friend to drive Lee to the airport. She seemed to be as excited as Lee was nervous. Both of them thought it was unreal that Lee was on her way to California to spend two weeks with a rock star. Debbie insisted Lee get lots of pictures of famous people, especially Eddie Brandon.

Debbie pulled the car up to the curb at the drop-off point and got out so she could give Lee a hug. "Have fun! I'll miss you!"

Lee hugged her back, feeling strangely disconnected already. "I'll miss you, too, but I'll be back before you know it. I'll only be gone for two weeks."

For some reason, Debbie hugged her extra hard one last time before letting her go.

CHAPTER TEN

Lee made her way through LAX in a sea of people. They came in every shape and size, and wore every conceivable style of dress. She feared she would never find Roddy in the mob milling around the baggage claim carousel.

Her eyes roved over the crowd, and suddenly she saw him. He must have already spotted her because he wore a huge grin, along with his torn-to-shreds jeans, a sleeveless black tee-shirt, and bright yellow aqua socks. He peeled away from the pillar he leaned against and made his way over in long strides.

He grasped her arms and kissed her quickly, then leaned back to simply stare. "You made it. I was afraid you wouldn't come."

She laughed. "I was afraid you wouldn't be here."

He frowned for a second, but then laughed. "I don't believe that. You walked into the room like you own the place."

"I must be a better actress than I thought. I've been a bundle of nerves since we talked."

He just stared at her for a few seconds, and then impulsively took her in his arms. Lee responded to his kiss with vigor and pressed herself against his hard length. Her lips were soft and responsive under his, and the all-encompassing need she felt for him rose up to overtake her.

He had an unreadable look in his eyes when he finally pulled away. He took her hand in his, though, and led her closer to the carousel. Lee pointed out her suitcase and he retrieved it for her, and then they were on their way.

Lee was not surprised to find Roddy had used valet parking at the airport, even though she hadn't known it existed until that day. He tossed her suitcase in the trunk when the car pulled up, opened her door, and then they roared away from the airport without a backward glance.

Lee didn't let his foot-to-the-floor driving bother her. She wanted them to be alone as much as Roddy apparently did. She didn't care what anyone else might think of her actions because she knew Roddy understood her. This thing between them required no explanation. It also apparently required no caution and no words; just satisfaction.

Roddy pushed a CD into the stereo, and Lee sat back to enjoy it. The music was hard and driving, from a band she had never heard before. She simply absorbed everything; the music, the blur of palm trees racing by, and the aura of Roddy O'Neill. Until that moment, she had not realized how much she missed him after he left.

Lee knew she would be stocking up on memories over the next couple of weeks. Roddy was a one-of-a-kind man, and she would never be able to forget him.

◌

Roddy was glad Lee didn't seem to feel like talking. It was a refreshing change of pace to be with a woman like her. She didn't need to fill the air with pointless chatter, and though he knew she was glad to be there, she was cool about it. She would never fawn over him, and he appreciated it anew every time he saw her. Since their first night together, she hadn't gushed about her feelings on anything, and had yet to make a comment about his impressive car. Her reticence just made him want her more.

With that thought firmly in mind, he drove them up into the hills and wound through the maze of streets that comprised Beverly Hills. He pulled into his winding driveway and killed the engine in front of the imposing, Spanish-style house. There was a fountain playing out front, and the gardeners trimmed bushes and mowed grass in the distance.

"Here we are," he announced as he opened his door.

He enjoyed the look on Lee's face as she absorbed their surroundings. "I guess we're not in Minnesota anymore."

"Isn't that supposed to be Kansas?

"If this was Oz. It's beautiful here, Roddy. I'm blown away. I don't know what I expected, but it wasn't this."

"Maybe a rathole in East LA?" he said with a chuckle.

She hit him playfully in the arm. "Maybe about ten years ago. I guess I pictured you living somewhere more ultra modern."

Roddy's eyebrows shot up. "I'm glad I disappointed you there."

"Me too. Now that I'm here, I can see that this suits you."

"I'm glad you approve." He just smiled at her, thinking that she seemed to fit perfectly into the picture, too.

"Do I ever get to see the inside?"

Roddy cracked a smile. "Of course. Unfortunately, all the footmen have the day off, so I have to carry your luggage." He walked back to the trunk and pulled her suitcase out, then indicated she should precede him to the front door.

Lee walked slowly toward the entrance, and Roddy laid an arm around her shoulders on the way. He opened the front door and followed her into the cool, tiled foyer, where he immediately dropped her suitcase on the floor.

He was about to take Lee into his arms when his housekeeper, Rosa, came into the room. He made quick introductions and answered Rosa's questions about his dinner preferences before the woman went back to the kitchen and he was again alone with Lee.

He wasted no time sweeping her into his arms. "I've been waiting all week for this," he said into her hair as he lifted her off her feet.

He carried her up the stairs and kicked his bedroom door open when they reached it. She laughed and clung to his neck, planting kisses under his ear all the while. Her hands pushed up under his shirt to feel the smooth expanse of his chest, and his lips tasted her neck as he felt her pulse beneath them.

Roddy would never forget the first time he made love in his own bed in his own house. Before Lee, there had never been another woman in his private sanctuary, and he was glad of it. The memories they made there were for them alone. Lee gave and gave of herself while she took everything he offered and more. Afterwards, Roddy felt drained and lay on his back while she softly trailed her fingertips over his flat stomach.

Despite the way things had been between them before, he had been unprepared for the intensity of the interlude. He didn't really have a clear recollection of anything from the moment he caught sight of her at the airport. From that moment, he had gone on auto-pilot, unable to think about anything but being with Lee. He had intended to lead her casually into one of his guest bedrooms and seduce her, and instead found himself playing Rhett Butler. He still couldn't believe he had carried her up the stairs and brought her mindlessly straight to his own bedroom, where he all but tore her clothes off in his urgency to have her.

"What are you thinking about?" he asked as he stroked her soft, golden hair.

She smiled and opened her eyes. "I haven't been able to think for at least a week," she admitted while her fingers drew circles around his navel. "I feel absolutely perfect," she added, "and suddenly very, very tired."

He smiled over the top of her head. "Me too," he agreed, thinking perfect was exactly the way to describe things the way they were just then.

Roddy supposed some people might find his music poetic, but despite the lyrics he wrote, until that moment, he had never felt particularly romantic. He could already hear the strains of a ballad starting in the back of his mind. If he wasn't so tired, he would have gotten up and grabbed his guitar.

He and Lee drifted off to sleep wrapped around each other with their legs tangled in his fine cotton sheets. He awakened some time later to find the sky had gone dark. Lee had an arm flung across his chest, and both her legs were wrapped around one of his. He had to crane his neck to see the clock.

It was two a.m. It was unlike him to fall asleep much before that hour, but he supposed these were some unusual circumstances. He had hardly slept in weeks, particularly after Lee agreed to come out for a visit, and he was exhausted. Certainly, making love to her like his life depended on it had contributed to the situation, as well.

Roddy decided he had better call Eddie before Eddie called him or simply showed up on his doorstep.

He carefully disentangled himself from Lee and the rumpled bedcovers and stepped into a pair of cutoff shorts. Not used to having to worry about waking someone else, he then padded out of his thickly carpeted bedroom, silently crept down the stairs, and finally felt like he could breathe normally again once he got out to the patio.

His back yard was huge, and sat on two levels. The top level, by the house, was all done in stone that surrounded an L-shaped swimming pool. If he walked down a flight of smooth stone steps to the left of the cabana, he would be standing on a large expanse of green lawn bordered by flowering plants and an adobe wall. There were two trees out in the yard he was exceedingly proud of. They were supposed to yield fruit of some sort, but if they did, the gardeners ate it all before he could guess what it was since he was often on the road.

Roddy settled into a deck chair next to the pool and reached for the phone he kept there. Truth to tell, he wasn't really in the mood to talk to Eddie just then. He knew his best friend would give him a hard time about Lee and try to make him admit to things he wasn't ready to discuss. He needed to talk to a comfortable, familiar person, though. His emotions were all over the place, and he just wanted to get his head straight instead of letting them carry him away. Besides, Eddie would probably call any minute if he didn't call him first.

The moment Eddie's phone was answered, Roddy realized he needn't have worried. It was obvious the guitar player was busy when a vacuous female voice came on the line.

"Hello!" Her voice screamed perky. Roddy envisioned a pretty girl, no older than nineteen, dancing around Eddie's living room in part of a bikini, lush curves bouncing with every movement.

He rarely found it necessary to be polite, so he simply said, "Get Eddie."

Eddie was on the line in seconds. "This better be important," he snarled.

"You seem to be enjoying your newfound

freedom," Roddy said on a laugh.

"Oh yeah," Eddie agreed wholeheartedly. "Since I haven't heard from you 'til now, I'll guess you've enjoyed losing yours."

Roddy shook his head and barked out a laugh. Eddie's taunts were getting old.

"I have a houseguest for a couple of weeks," he insisted. "That's not the same as giving up my freedom."

Eddie's laugh held genuine amusement. "Two weeks, huh? Somehow I don't think the other half of that ticket is ever going to get used."

"You're only saying that because you want my five hundred bucks."

"Could be. I'd be willing to put a million on it that she stays longer than that, but you know me. I have no appreciation for an unearned fortune. I'd just blow your money on frivolous things."

Roddy's laugh was a little forced. "Awfully sure of yourself, aren't you?"

"Sure am. I'd hate to see you have to mortgage your house over a bet."

Sometimes, Roddy wished Eddie was there just so he could hit him. There were times he wasn't sure why he called him his best friend. Eddie Brandon really knew how to get on his nerves.

"What makes you so cocky about it?" Roddy wanted to know.

"Where is she now?"

"Sleeping."

"In your bed, right?" Eddie's question was more of an accusation. They both knew Roddy never let women invade the sanctity of his own bedroom. How Eddie knew Lee was already there was uncanny.

Still, Roddy was defensive. "So?"

"You don't share your space. Today, she's in your bed. Tomorrow, her clothes will be in your closet, and before long, her toothbrush will be permanently parked next to yours."

Perturbed, Roddy ran a hand through his hair. "What makes you so sure?" he asked almost plaintively.

He had the sinking feeling Eddie was right about all of it. Already, he honestly wasn't sure if he would be able to send Lee home in two weeks, just as Eddie had predicted.

"I've been there myself," Eddie said with surety. "Of course, that was with Claire, who isn't half the woman Lee is, and I wasn't goofy in love with her, but the situation is basically the same. Once you start breaking your rules with a woman, it's all over for you."

All Roddy heard him say was that Claire wasn't half the woman Lee was, and he wondered how Eddie knew that, too. He had never really looked upon Eddie as someone possessing great wisdom, but he was dead-on with everything that day, and Roddy wanted to know how he was figuring it all out.

"She ignored me," was his simple, patient explanation. "Do you know how long it's been since a woman ignored me?"

"I guess she likes my type better," Roddy said with a shrug.

"You don't believe that any more than I do,"

Eddie chuckled. "Or you wouldn't be breaking your rules."

"What rules are those, exactly?" Roddy was getting annoyed with Eddie's calm assurances that he was a doomed man.

"Let's see," Eddie began, "first off, you let her spend the whole night with you, *after* you brought her to a party with the band, which is something you vowed a long time ago you'd never do. Then, you went back to her. You drove a total of five days to spend a weekend with her. And then you brought her here, to your house, when you could just as easily have put her up in a hotel. But she's not just in your house. Even though you pointed out you've got all those guest rooms, she's in your bedroom, in your bed."

"Have you been writing all this down?" Roddy scowled.

Eddie's response was near-maniacal laughter. "Rod, when your closest friend goes over the edge, you notice."

"Yeah, well, maybe you should go notice your little bimbo."

He hung up when Eddie laughed at him again.

He knew he was getting angry with Eddie simply because he was right. Roddy really had gone over the edge from the moment he noticed Lee across a crowded room. He was simply diving deeper and deeper into his own self-made pit every time he broke another one of his long-standing rules for her. Eddie seemed to think it was all over, and his mother apparently thought it was absolutely wonderful.

So why couldn't he be happy about it? Why not just accept it?

Uncomfortably, Roddy realized it was because he was a world-famous, millionaire rock star. He was supposed to be impervious to the emotional turmoil normal people felt. He was jaded, which it was impossible not to be when girls threw themselves at him every time he stepped outside. Even Lee had not told him no.

What made her different, though, was the way she said yes. She wanted him because he was Roddy O'Neill the man, not Roddy O'Neill the rock star. She responded to his kiss and his touch because of *him*, not for his image, money, or fame. He knew she had nothing to gain from their encounter, and had only slept with him to please herself, even though she expected their relationship to last no more than a couple of hours. She asked him for nothing, and wouldn't even tell him her name. She was a rare find indeed.

So, now she was there, sleeping in Roddy's bed. He already knew he wanted her to stay. In that moment, he realized the two-week vacation was a ploy he had concocted to fool himself.

He wondered if she realized it, and suddenly worried he would not be able to convince her to stay. He knew she would not want to be kept by him; she was independent and proud. He supposed he could suggest she find a job, but knew it wasn't a viable solution. He certainly wasn't going to take money from her for rent and bills, and the moment the paparazzi got wind of her, they would hound her until she got fired or quit. The two of them could figure something out, he was sure, but in the interim, he had to make her see things his way. It came as somewhat of a surprise, but he realized he wanted to take care of her.

Roddy lit a cigarette and stared up at the sky. He could no longer lie to himself, but it might not be so easy to bring Lee around to his way of thinking.

CHAPTER ELEVEN

Lee awakened the next morning with California sun straining to get past the curtains in Roddy's bedroom. Roddy lay stretched out on the bed beside her, one leg proprietarily thrown over hers, and his fingers were tangled in her hair. As this was the first time she had seen him sleeping, she took the opportunity to study him.

Like most people, he looked innocent in sleep. All worries were erased from his features. His mouth looked soft and sensual, and she remembered the feel of it on her skin. After taking the time to admire his face, she let her eyes travel downward, first stopping at his tattoos. They seemed to take on a life of their own on the sleeping man, and she wondered what had prompted him to acquire them. She knew at least one of them had been there since his not-so-innocent youth, and she smiled and let her eyes move on. They followed his sinewy arms, skimmed over his smooth chest, and paused again to admire his legs. They were muscular, but not big, attached to lean hips that moved in all the right ways. Lee was certain she would never tire of him.

Unfortunately, in all likelihood, he would soon tire

of her. Lee had followed his escapades in magazine articles for years, and knew he was not a one-woman man. She didn't expect him to change his ways just for her, as well as she knew she wouldn't settle for less than a whole relationship with any man. Eventually, Roddy would crave variety, and that would mean the end.

She gave herself a mental shake. There was no point in letting her mind go there. She was in Beverly Hills for a two-week vacation, and once she flew home, that would really be the end of things between her and Roddy O'Neill. It was pointless to think about anything beyond those two weeks.

Of its own accord, her right hand reached out to very gently stroke his thigh, the moves almost involuntary. She had to smile when Roddy's body immediately responded to her touch, and she nuzzled into his shoulder and simply stared at him.

Lee didn't realize he was awake until, with his eyes still closed, his lips sought hers while his arms curled around her. She enjoyed the feel of just kissing him for awhile, until he covered her body with his and finally plunged into her. They moved together, stoking the fire between them to a fever pitch. Lee felt herself taken higher and higher, closer and closer to the precipice, when Roddy suddenly stopped.

Her body strained and writhed beneath him, and her eyes flew open to gaze hungrily into his. What she saw there nearly pushed her over the edge on its own.

Roddy rested on his elbows above her, still locked inside her, and brought his face to within inches of hers. "We need to talk," he said evenly, as if they were sitting across the dinner table from one another. Only the look in his eyes betrayed him.

Lee wrapped her legs more tightly around him, as if he would attempt to get away. "Right now?"

He kept staring down at her. "I can't think of a better time when we've got something serious to discuss."

Her response was to bury her fingers in his hair and look deeply into his eyes. She held hers level with them as he spoke again.

"I don't want you to go." He said it so quietly, she would not have heard him if they were further apart.

"I'm not going anywhere right now."

"I don't want you to go anywhere ever."

"What?"

He laughed a little, which seemed almost painful. "I mean, I don't want you to go home. I want this to be more than a vacation. I want you to stay with me."

Lee was afraid for a moment she would faint. She blinked a couple of times to make sure she wasn't dreaming, and then caught his gaze again. "Why are you asking me this now?"

He smiled and shifted his hips just a bit. "Because if you say yes, I'm in the perfect position to celebrate. But if you say no, I can try to coerce you into saying yes."

Her legs tightened around him. "You fight dirty."

His eyes darkened. "Just give me an answer, Lee. I want you to stay. I don't want you to worry about money and who pays for what. And I don't want to hear about kept women. I just want you to be with me, and right now the only way it's going to work is if you let me take care of you."

She was stunned, but he obviously wasn't giving her a chance to think it over, which she supposed was the point. He just poised above her, waiting for her answer.

Lee had a short argument with herself. It took less than a second for it to sink in that Roddy wanted her to stay. While that made her giddy, she did not want to be anyone's kept woman. It would seem a little odd to go out and get a lousy job with a paltry paycheck, which was all she was qualified for, while living in Roddy's palatial mansion, though. And how would she get there? On the bus? She doubted if they even allowed buses on Roddy's street. If she wanted to be honest with herself, she enjoyed independence, but did not really love her job. It was what she did to keep a roof over her head, but it did not really fulfill her. She did not envision working in the library until retirement. On the other hand, being with Roddy made her feel truly alive for the first time in her life. It was easy to picture waking up beside him every morning and falling asleep in his arms every night.

If she wanted to be honest with herself, being with Roddy was all she really wanted, no matter what.

"I have one stipulation before I'll agree," she said after a long pause.

Roddy swallowed and shifted a little again, a reminder that he wasn't above using unfair tactics to get his way. "What?"

Lee's eyes were very serious as they bored into his.

"I won't stay with you if there are other women. I can't live that way."

He buried his face in the soft cloud of her hair and wrapped his arms tightly around her. "I don't want anyone else, Lee. I haven't even looked at another woman since the night we met, and I certainly haven't touched anyone. It's only been you since then, I swear it."

He was so serious, she let go of her doubts and smiled at last.

"Okay," she agreed, throwing her pride and independence to the winds. It was worth it if she could follow her heart's desire, and she felt unbelievably happy and free as she did so.

Roddy simply stared at her for several seconds, and then he kissed her to the point of distraction. His hips began moving again, rebuilding the fires and sealing the pact that made her his. Lee gave herself up with total abandon, carrying him along on her tidal wave of passion, and they crashed together in ecstasy.

Lee smiled to herself as he held her afterwards, and hoped they could hold all their serious discussions in a similar manner.

ଔ

They were barely out of bed when Roddy urged Lee to call Mr. Eggers with the news. Her boss expressed disappointment, but told her he knew something was afoot from the day she came back to work after the concert. Lee knew he noticed she had changed after that night, and understood he wasn't very thrilled about it. Even though he wished her happiness, he would have been more enthusiastic if she hadn't run off with the likes of Roddy O'Neill.

Debbie, of course, was excited enough for three people. She immediately offered to dispose of Lee's apartment and everything in it, between breathless congratulations.

"Congratulations aren't really necessary," Lee said mildly. "I'm not getting married. And I've got enough in my savings to keep my rent paid for awhile. I think I'll hold onto the apartment for now."

"Oh." Debbie sounded bewildered. "Why?"

"Just in case," was Lee's vague response. She didn't really want to put her worst fears into words. "Please take my plants, though. There aren't many."

"Sure." Debbie sounded a bit distracted, no doubt wondering why Lee would want to keep a tiny apartment in Minneapolis when she now lived in the lap of luxury in Beverly Hills. "I hope you won't forget about me."

"Of course I won't!" Lee said firmly. "You're my best friend."

Despite the small bit of doubt that prompted her to keep her apartment for awhile, she felt incredibly good about the world at large. The months of loneliness and pining for Roddy were over. They were together now because he wanted her to stay.

❧

Roddy was thrilled Lee had so easily agreed to move in. Somehow over the past few months of her absence, she had become incredibly important. Now that he had her, he did not want to lose her until he was damn good and ready.

He didn't believe his current euphoric state of

mind would last, but there was no reason to let Lee in on that. He would see to it she was well provided for when the time came for her to move on. Since she had given up her job and her home to be with him, he could do nothing less.

Roddy didn't understand why he already felt sort of guilty about it. There was no reason for that. He hadn't made Lee any lasting promises, and she hadn't asked him to. She knew the score, and the rules of the game. Hadn't she been playing it like an expert since the night they met? If she stayed true to form, he wouldn't have anything to worry about. Just because she was moving in didn't mean she would start making all sorts of demands. Lee would keep things in perspective because she was too smart to actually fall in love with a womanizing jerk like him, wasn't she?

Roddy decided he didn't really want to think about that sort of thing right then. He was far too happy. There was a beautiful woman sharing his bed who wasn't a model, actress, or singer, and she wasn't even aspiring to be one. She was simply warm, giving, and passionate. Every man on earth wanted what Roddy O'Neill now had, and he wasn't going to spoil his good fortune by worrying about where it was going in the future.

They spent their first few days together doing almost nothing. They lay by the pool and made love for hours on end, and got to know each other a little more. Roddy was thrilled that she settled into his home so easily, and knew with more certainty each day that asking her to stay had been the right decision.

He wasn't used to such inactivity, though, and after a couple of days of it, he felt restless. It was time to get back to work. Despite their attempts to make light of his situation, the band was impatient to get back to business. Roddy had to admit he was beginning to feel that way himself. Eddie had been absolutely right about Lee being able to cure what ailed him, but now that she had done so, he was itching to get back into the thick of things.

Without knowing why it was so important, since he certainly wasn't in love, Roddy worried about Lee's reaction when he broke the news. She would be left alone for several hours a day when he returned to work, and he didn't know how she would feel about it. Roddy had angered many women with his careless behavior in the past, but when they didn't like what he did, his reaction had always been to smile and tell them to find another man. He knew he would never say anything of the sort to Lee, probably because she would simply leave without a backward glance.

Roddy chose a quiet moment to broach the subject of work. They were relaxing together on a chaise after taking an afternoon swim, and the radio played softly in the background when he turned to her with a rather grave expression.

Always sensitive to his moods, Lee frowned and asked, "What's wrong?"

"Nothing, I hope," he told her with a smile. "It's just that you might not like what I have to say."

Lee's frown deepened, and he could already see her mind starting to sort through unpleasant possibilities. "Spit it out," she ordered on a sigh.

Roddy gulped and feared the worst. "The last few days have been great, but I...uh...I have to go back to work."

"And?"

"I won't be able to spend so much time with you anymore." Roddy let out a long, shaky breath. "I want to show you the studio and stuff, of course, but if I'm going to really work, I won't be able to have you there every day."

"And you're afraid I'll have a problem with that?"

"Well...yeah."

Roddy was flatly surprised at her incredulous look. He had frankly expected some sort of tantrum. He thought he would hear something along the lines of: *Why can't you take me with you? I won't be in the way. I promise. I'll just sit in the background and watch, and you won't even know I'm there.*

Instead, Lee simply said, "Roddy," and covered his hand with hers. "It's so sweet that you're concerned about me being here alone, but I know you have to work. I know your career is demanding, and that sometimes you'll even have to leave town without me. Believe it or not, I took that into consideration when I agreed to stay here. I was actually surprised that you've spent so much time with me over the past few days."

Roddy was just floored. "You were?"

If he was given to such notions, he would start to believe God had made Lee just for him.

Lee just smiled. "Of course. I know you're a busy man. I've read everything I could get my hands on about you for years."

A slow, pleased smile spread over Roddy's features. "You're not afraid you'll get bored? I know you don't know anyone out here."

"Roddy, this is LA. Hollywood. Beverly Hills. Rodeo Drive. How could I be bored here? I'm from Minneapolis, remember?"

"Minneapolis isn't that bad."

"It's a great city, if it's not winter," she agreed. "But the whole LA scene is new to me, so I'm actually kind of excited to go out and explore it."

Roddy lay there in contentment for awhile, immensely pleased with life at large, until another thing occurred to him.

"I just thought of something else you aren't gonna like," he said as he turned to face Lee again.

"Oh?" She arched a brow.

"There's more to rock and roll than the studio. I have to get out and create some publicity sometimes, too."

"And?"

"We're going to have to go to parties and premieres and all that."

She threw a hand over her eyes in mock distress. "Oh, please, anything but that!"

"And photographers will follow us around."

She sobered instantly. "Really?"

"Not everywhere. Just when they see us before we see them."

Lee looked doubtful now. "I'm not so sure about that. Why would anyone want to take my picture? I'm just a library clerk from Minneapolis. I don't want to be in the limelight."

Roddy smiled, certain he knew the way around her objections. "I suppose you could just stay cloistered up here all the time. We don't have to go out together. You'd be my little secret."

Lee actually seemed to consider it for a second, until she noticed the look in his eyes. His suggestion was not serious; it was a dare. Though he would allow her to stay hidden if she wanted, he already knew she would not. She would fully be a part of his life if she was going to be in it at all, and he knew it.

She wrinkled her nose. "I love it here, Roddy, but I can't stay hidden away from the world. I guess I'll learn how to deal with the paparazzi."

He cocked a teasing eyebrow. "Only if you're sure."

She shoved him off the chaise and into the pool, then followed him in, and they abandoned serious discussions for the next little while.

ଔ

The next morning, while Lee still lay in bed, Roddy gave her two little wrapped packages. The uncertain look on his face made her afraid to open them, but she couldn't refuse.

The first little box held a credit card with her name on it.

"That's yours," Roddy informed her in a no-nonsense tone. "You can use it whenever you need something, want something, or if you're just bored."

Lee just stared at the little rectangle of plastic. If she took it, she would truly be a card-carrying, kept woman.

"Roddy, I don't know," she murmured. "It's

sweet of you, but I feel so…"

"Ssh," he silenced her with a gentle finger over her lips. "I know we didn't really talk about this when you agreed to stay, but it's part of the deal. I had your name put on it, so nobody but us and my accountant will know who pays the bills. I know you worry about that kind of stuff, but I really don't care about the money. I don't think any less of you today than I did when you had a job. And this is how it always used to be before women started having careers."

"I know, but…"

"Besides," he cut her off, "you need new clothes. I like everything you brought with you, and it's fine for hanging out here, but you're gonna need some new stuff when I take you out. It's all about image in LA, and I can't have anyone making comments on my girlfriend's clothes."

Lee just stared at him for a moment. Unfortunately, he had a point. Since he had warned her about the paparazzi, she had noticed that sections of magazines and portions of entertainment programs were often devoted to what people were wearing. Even if she had a job, she doubted she could afford the kind of clothes she saw on celebrities. The last thing she wanted to do was embarrass Roddy by looking like a fashion-impaired doofus from a flyover state.

Roddy pushed the card into her palm. "Go out, find a few stores, and buy whatever you want to be photographed in. You're doing it for me, you know. Even I tweak my image a little when I go out."

Lee allowed him to curl her fingers around the

credit card, but she sighed. "Maybe I'll take you up on your offer to let me be a recluse."

Roddy shook his head with a smile. "That window of opportunity is already closed, and I didn't really mean it anyway. You're gorgeous, babe. I *want* to be seen with you."

Lee flushed. "Are you serious?"

He took her chin in his hand and tipped it so their eyes met. "Of course I am. I could have tried to keep you in the background if I wanted to, but that wouldn't make you happy."

"I guess not. It probably would have made me go back home."

He smiled now. "Probably. So, you see, you're just going to have to bend a little bit. You're not a librarian in Minneapolis anymore. You're Roddy O'Neill's sexy girlfriend."

She laughed along with him, realizing he was right. Quite frankly, she had never enjoyed the conservative style of dress forced upon her at the library. She just got used to it. Lee supposed she would probably take to her new role like a fish to water. If she and Roddy lasted long enough, it would probably become a part of her, just like Roddy's wardrobe and tattoos were such an integral part of him.

She accepted the credit card at last. "I don't know what to buy."

"Whatever you want," he said. "Buy things that please you, not what you think I'll like. I trust your taste, and I want you to be comfortable. This is LA, but I still want you to be you."

"Don't say I didn't warn you," she threatened

quite seriously.

Roddy just laughed and kissed her, and then pushed the other package she had forgotten into her hands. She stared balefully at it for a moment before slipping the ribbon off, and her eyebrows shot up to her hairline when a set of car keys fell into her hands.

Lee's eyes cut to his. "What are these for?"

He took them from her and held them to his chest. "My car."

"You're giving me your car?"

He smiled. "No. It's a symbol."

"I could argue that if I was greedy."

Roddy laughed in genuine amusement.

"I hope you're not buying me a Maserati," Lee said as she crossed her arms over her chest.

"I will if you want one," he said in all seriousness. "The insurance would be hell on two of them, but you can have whatever you want."

Lee sighed and had to look away for a moment. Her expression was prim when she turned back to Roddy. "I am not allowing you to spend that much money on me for anything."

"I had a feeling you'd take that attitude," he said with a grin. "That's why I haven't bought your car yet. I thought I'd let you pick one out."

Lee felt like she was going to cry for a moment, but the look on Roddy's face held her in check. He wasn't trying to paint her into a corner, she knew. He was trying to take care of her, like he promised he would, and she should be happy. Most women would be ecstatic in her position, and she needed to get with the program.

"I don't need a car."

"Don't you have a license?"

"Of course I do!"

"Then you need a car. This is LA. Everyone has one."

It was true. One didn't have to be from Los Angeles to know that.

Roddy was obviously tired of her objections and went on as if she hadn't voiced any. "Tell me what you want, and what color, and I'll have it delivered tomorrow."

"Just like that?"

Roddy tossed the keys on the floor and wrapped his arms around her, rolling them over on the bed until she was on top of him. "Yep. Time to get used to the rock star lifestyle, Lee."

She rolled her eyes. "You're spoiling me rotten."

"You deserve it."

"I do not."

Roddy rolled them back over until she was under him again. "Yes, you do. You have no idea what it was like before you came out here. I couldn't write a damn thing. I wrote a song about you on the tour, and then...nothing."

"You wrote a song about me?"

He ignored her question and went on. "The guys were getting ready to bail on me, and even I was starting to think I had lost it. Eddie told me I should bring you out here, and the minute you showed up, music started coming to me again. I need you, Lee. Right now, I wouldn't have a career without you."

"Oh, please." Lee knew he was exaggerating more

than a little bit.

"I'm serious. I'm not ready to retire, but it was scary when I couldn't write. I've never had that problem before." His eyes darkened. "You changed something in me, Lee. Nothing matters anymore without you, so please, let me share my stuff with you."

It was hard to put forth any more objections when he said it like that. Lee didn't fool herself into thinking she was in any way responsible for his success, but she agreed with one thing Roddy told her. Nothing seemed to matter anymore except being with him.

CHAPTER TWELVE

Roddy ended rehearsal early. The band liked his new song a lot, and they had already started working with it. Roddy liked to wrap up a session early when things were going well. It meant everyone would return to the studio with an upbeat attitude and the next session would also be productive. He wouldn't admit to anyone in the band that he also wanted to get home early so he could see Lee.

There was always a fly in the ointment, though, and Roddy had not been able to shake Eddie after rehearsal. Eddie was in a mood because of a premiere they were to attend that night. The movie featured one of the band's songs, and the video for it would play during the opening credits. It was quite a coup for the band, and a major honor. But because of it, Eddie would not leave Roddy alone. He stuck to him like glue all day, even going so far as to follow him home so they could arrive at the premiere at the same time.

Roddy wasn't fooled. Eddie was curious about Lee. He knew that night would be her first public appearance with Roddy, and he didn't want to miss a minute of the excitement. It made Roddy feel a little bit like he and Lee were going to the prom, but he could not exclude Eddie. Without a family of his own to hover over, Roddy got his attention by default.

"Lee!" Roddy called out the moment they walked in the door.

There was no response.

Roddy turned a little nervously to Eddie. "She must be out back."

He had to force himself to saunter through the house, rather than charging like a bull. He was glad he maintained control when they did not find Lee out back. It was Rosa's day off, so he couldn't ask her where Lee had gone, and he began to worry. Lee was always right there, waiting for him when he got home, no matter the hour, and it bothered him that she was gone when they had plans for the night.

Honestly, though, he wasn't really worried about the premiere. He just missed seeing Lee after a long day of work. He had already gotten used to the way she greeted him every day with a smile before he mixed them drinks out by the pool. They then sat and talked about whatever they had done that day before going in to eat the meal Rosa always prepared for them. Roddy enjoyed their conversations because Lee never talked about silly things, like finding the right sizes when she shopped. She usually had funny anecdotes about her encounters with other people, or wry observations about the state of the world. Roddy felt like a vital part of his day was missing since she wasn't there.

He also admitted to disappointment because he

wanted to show her off to Eddie. Though he never slept with them, Eddie was fascinated by intelligent, witty women. The guitar player was unfortunately convinced that sexy and smart did not go together, and Roddy wanted to prove him wrong while he enjoyed his bragging rights. Since Lee wasn't there, he supposed it would have to wait.

"Make yourself a drink," he suggested to Eddie, heading for the stairs. "I'm going to see if she's sleeping."

Roddy took the steps three at a time. He was starting to get nervous about Lee. She had only ventured out in her new car a few times, and she still wasn't familiar with Los Angeles. It was entirely possible she was lost or had been in an accident. She didn't have a cell phone yet, which he vowed to fix the very next day, so he had no way to contact her. But before he worked himself into a lather, he wanted to make sure she wasn't merely taking a nap.

He tried to take the last few steps in one leap and missed. He was glad Eddie wasn't there to see him sprawl on the floor, because he would have burst a seam on his jeans laughing. Now hoping Lee wasn't there to witness his clumsiness, he picked himself off the floor and walked more casually into his bedroom.

Lee wasn't there, or in the bathroom. Instead, a wet towel lay on the floor, and there was lipstick all over the mirror.

Apparently, Lee had left him a message. How like her to do it with flamboyance, instead of just scribbling a note on a piece of paper or leaving a voicemail. She also didn't follow any Hollywood clichés, and instead of leaving a message of one or two words, she had scrawled an entire paragraph that covered the entire mirror from top to bottom. He hoped Rosa would forgive her.

The message read:

Roddy, if you get back before me, I'm still out shopping. I had to find something nice for our first important date! I'll get back as soon as I can, but you know LA traffic even better than I do. By the way, your new snakeskin pants were delivered today. Rrrrr! Can't wait to see how they look. They're in a box on the bed. Lee

She had left a lip print next to her name, and just looking at it got him all hot and bothered. He no longer had to worry, but he still could not wait until she got home.

Roddy O'Neill wasn't used to waiting for anything. If he asked for something or made demands, someone immediately gave him what he wanted. Even Lee had not disappointed him thus far. Perhaps it was indicative of an incurable sickness, but Roddy found waiting for Lee and the attendant anticipation of her arrival to be intoxicating indeed.

He slipped easily into a fantasy scene of lounging by the pool with Eddie wherein Lee suddenly appeared in the doorway to the house with a shopping bag dangling from her fingers. Eddie's mouth would naturally fall open at how beautiful she was, especially since Eddie didn't have a clear recollection of her and tended to picture all girls with brains as dull and mousy. Lee would say, "Hi, Eddie," in her sultry voice and then completely forget him as she approached Roddy. At that point, the picture misted over and his body began to take over the vision, until he jerked himself back to the present.

He wondered if everyone sat around indulging in such fantasies, but then decided he better stop standing around thinking about it.

Roddy found Eddie out on the patio with a drink, and told him, "I guess she's still out shopping."

Eddie cocked a brow. "Gee, I hope she makes it home okay. I'm really worried."

Roddy couldn't miss his sarcasm. "Shut up."

He was really running out of patience with Eddie. The guitar player had been a Class A pain in the rear all day. He had refused to let up on giving Roddy a hard time about his appearance, and even suggested he should spiff up a little bit for the premiere, since it was such an important occasion. Roddy resented his overbearing interference, but knew he was mostly annoyed because he wanted to be alone with Lee. Now that Lee wasn't even there, it was irksome that Eddie had the nerve to laugh at him.

Knowing Eddie would just rile him more, he let it go and decided to talk about less incendiary things like the new record, their new video, and the movie being premiered. They had plenty of time before they needed to leave for the festivities, so they sat back and sipped at cold drinks while they waited for Lee.

Considerable time had passed by the time Eddie glanced at his watch. "I don't know about you, but I should probably start getting ready to go," he said.

Roddy also noticed the time and set his drink down. Worry about Lee crept back into his consciousness. "Yeah, me too, I guess."

Neither of them mentioned his missing girlfriend as they peeled out of their deck chairs and made their way into the house.

Roddy told himself to shake off his dejection when the front door suddenly flew open and Lee came careening through with an armload of shopping bags.

"I'm sorry I'm late," she said through heavy breaths. "They had to make a couple of adjustments and it took forever."

It wasn't the scene Roddy had envisioned, but since it was real, it was better. Lee looked absolutely delectable standing there wearing painted-on jeans with her hair in wild, gold disarray. Her tee-shirt clung enticingly to her skin, and Roddy was about to drag her upstairs for their usual greeting when Eddie rounded the corner and got singed by the heat radiating from the two of them.

"Oh good, Lee's here," Eddie said cheerfully, his voice working like a bucket of cold water on both of them. "Reintroduce us, Rod."

"You remember Eddie?" Roddy asked, stepping back a little.

Lee collected herself nicely. "Hi, Eddie. Of course I remember you." She shoved the handles of a shopping bag up one arm and extended her hand.

Eddie raised a brow at Roddy but took it and gave it a perfunctory shake. "Nice to see you again," he said in a show of manners Roddy rarely saw. The way he looked her up and down was anything but polite, though. "Roddy should have taken you out earlier than this. He's been hoarding you to himself for way too long."

Lee smiled easily at his flattery and turned to Roddy. "You didn't tell me Eddie had a charming streak."

"I didn't know," Roddy said in response, earning a scowl from Eddie. His eyes laughed down into Lee's. They both knew she felt compelled to be especially cool toward Eddie because he fully expected to be able to pique her interest somehow. It warmed Roddy immensely to know it would never happen since Lee only had eyes for him.

"Shouldn't we all get dressed and head for the ball?" Eddie snapped, obviously a little uncomfortable with the intimacy between them.

Lee glanced up at a clock on the wall and winced. "I know I should. I better get moving."

She gathered her packages and dashed off up the stairs, leaving Roddy to shrug his shoulders at Eddie before the two of them followed.

Lee had told Roddy her dress was a surprise, and she was getting ready in one of the guest rooms down the hall from the master suite so he wouldn't see her until her look was complete. Roddy already missed her when he shut his bedroom door, and decided it was a good idea to take a cold shower before he got dressed to go.

❧

Eddie whistled under his breath as he shut himself into the room he kept at Roddy's house. Things were more serious with Roddy and Lee than even he had imagined. The electricity between them was palpable, and he was afraid he might suffer severe burns if he accidentally stepped between them. Roddy was blind to everything but her, and she seemed to suffer a similar affliction over him.

He grimaced at their domestic bliss, certain it had never been that way between himself and Claire. Roddy and Lee were almost nauseatingly happy together.

Lee sure was a looker. Even casually dressed in jeans and a tee-shirt she took his breath away. Though she hailed from Minnesota, she looked like the quintessential California girl with her sun-kissed skin and golden locks, not to mention the body he was certain had never been defiled by a plastic surgeon's scalpel. If Roddy wasn't so obviously gone for her, Eddie would have pulled out all the stops himself.

"Damn it!" he suddenly heard her yell through the wall separating the rooms where they dressed.

He smirked, used to domestic instability, and turned back to the mirror to inspect his appearance. Eddie's long, brown-black hair fell naturally in a wild mane. His black leather pants couldn't have been tighter without permanently crippling him in some way. He wasn't wearing a shirt, just an unbuttoned black leather vest over his smooth chest. He carefully laid a black leather cowboy hat over his hair, winked at his image, and smiled. He looked hot, if his own opinion was anything to go by.

Mid-smile, he heard a timid knock at the door. Thinking it was probably Rosa, he sauntered over and flung it open. He would never forget the vision that confronted him on the other side.

Lee stood there in an incredible creation of yellow

leather and feathers. She had yet to don her shoes, so she seemed shorter than he remembered, since Eddie wore his boots. He watched her toes curl in the carpet as her eyes spit fire and brimstone.

"Can I come in for a second?" Her polite tone belied the angry look on her face.

Eddie stepped back in astonishment, wondering how to act. Why was she there? Had the yelling been a fight with Roddy? Was she coming on to him? What should he do?

"This damn thing is supposed to fit!" she hissed when he shut the door.

"What?" Eddie just gaped at her in confusion.

"The dress!" she snapped. "I can't get the stupid zipper more than halfway up and I can't ask Roddy to help me because I want to surprise him, and he's not supposed to see me 'til I'm dressed. Rosa's not here, and I had nowhere else to go. Can you help me?"

She turned to show him her partially-exposed back with its half-done zipper. Eddie got a view of nothing but her shoulder blades, but he still turned his head and zipped her up as quickly as possible.

The moment her dress cooperated, Lee's mood changed, and she whipped back around to face him with a smile this time.

"How do I look?" she asked, obviously wanting an honest answer and not just a compliment.

Eddie gulped. "Roddy better have industrial-strength seams on his pants."

Lee's yellow dress was skin-tight leather that stopped a few inches past her hips. The dress could probably have kick-started her career as a model with the way it clung to her skin and pushed her breasts provocatively toward the sweetheart neckline. The sleeves were a profusion of bright yellow feathers that fluttered halfway to her elbows. She wore dramatic eye make-up, and her lips were a traffic-stopping red. Lee hadn't needed to do much with her hair, though. Apparently, flipping her head a couple times and hair-spraying the results was all it took to make it red-carpet ready.

Utterly unaware of the effect she had on him, she gave Eddie a tentative smile. "You look great, Eddie. No date tonight?"

"She's coming with the car," he said, attempting to sound casual and unaffected.

Considering his unexpected reaction to Lee, he was glad he and Roddy were traveling in separate vehicles. Until he could convince his hormones that Lee was strictly off-limits, he knew it would be best to keep his distance from her.

The smile Lee gave him was devoid of guile. "Thanks for your help. I'll see you downstairs."

Eddie had never been happier to close the door on a beautiful woman. No wonder Roddy had not flinched at losing five hundred bucks over her.

※

Roddy glanced at his image in the mirror. He didn't think he looked too bad in his new snakeskin pants with a wide belt slung low over his hips. He had tucked a white silk shirt into the waistband, but had only done up a couple of the buttons. His usual bandanna had been replaced by a swath of dark red silk in a black paisley pattern to match his boots. The overall effect was pure rock and roll, but Roddy still sometimes envied Eddie his pretty-boy looks. It got tiresome having magazines put him down in comparison to the band's lead guitar player. He thought he always looked better when he smiled, though, and he had plenty of reasons for that these days. As long as he could remember to keep a smile pasted to his face, they wouldn't be able to trash him too much.

"Not bad," was Eddie's assessment from the doorway.

Roddy raised a caustic brow at him in the mirror. "What? No complaints about my hair even? You aren't afraid to be seen with me?" He turned to give Eddie a hard time about his outfit, but froze when he saw the almost haunted look on his friend's face.

"What?" Roddy wanted to know.

"Nothing," Eddie said vaguely. "Lee's waiting for you downstairs."

Roddy smiled to himself, thinking things were right back where they belonged. "Does she look okay?"

"You could say that."

Eddie announced he wanted to make a couple phone calls before they took off, so he went back to his room and Roddy made his way downstairs to join Lee.

He first spotted a pair of yellow shoes with impossibly high heels. His eyes slowly traveled upward, admiring Lee's calves and thighs before the yellow leather began. The visual trip ended when he reached Lee's face, framed by her wild gold hair and lit up by a confident smile.

She was perfection. Roddy knew she would be the envy of all the starlets attending the premiere. In that dress, her picture was sure to be taken more often than theirs. Lee could make the lame get up and walk in her ensemble, he was sure. He smiled to himself as he realized nobody would comment on his looks as long as he was next to Lee. They were even likely to steal some attention away from Eddie.

"You look great," Lee said to Roddy as she admired the fit of his snakeskin pants with his boots.

"Maybe almost good enough to be seen with you," he replied. "Nobody's gonna believe I stole you from a library."

Two limousines pulled into Roddy's driveway, and a blonde in a tight satin dress alighted from one and approached the front door to ring the bell. Her mouth fell open when Lee answered.

"Um, I'm here to meet Eddie Brandon?" Her eyes seemed unsure.

Lee opened the door. "He'll be down in a minute," she said as she let the other woman in. "Would you like a drink or something while you wait?"

Comprehension seemed to dawn when the woman spied Roddy casually leaned against the banister. No doubt she had been thinking Eddie had double-booked his dates until she spotted him.

"I'm Lee Miller, and I'm sure you know Roddy O'Neill," Lee said when the other woman declined her drink offer.

Mention of his name was all their visitor needed to

change her whole demeanor from uncertain to sultry. "I love your music," she cooed on the introduction.

"Thanks." Roddy turned to whisper in Lee's ear, "Don't worry, she'll be gone by tomorrow."

She was saved from having to make any kind of reply when Eddie swaggered down the stairs. His expression was one of both relief and disappointment when he spied his date waiting for him in the front hall. Roddy knew Eddie had to be thinking the same thing he was: the other woman paled next to Lee.

"You've met everyone, Bambi?" Eddie breezed through the introductions.

Roddy turned to Lee, and they both incredulously mouthed, *Bambi?* at each other, both suddenly beset by a fit of nearly uncontrollable giggles.

Roddy sternly got hold of himself and took Lee's hand. "Is everyone ready to head out?"

"It's getting late," Lee piped up. "We should go."

He looked down into her face, searching for some trace of nerves, and found none. He gave her a reassuring smile nonetheless and led her out to the car. Eddie followed with Bambi glued to his side, not looking as pleased with himself as he usually did.

Once they got to the premiere, Lee glanced curiously out the windows at everything. She still outwardly betrayed no sign of nerves, but Roddy remembered he had been strung tight the first time he attended something like this.

Moments before it was time to alight from the car, he handed Lee a pair of oversized sunglasses. "Put these on or you'll go blind," he warned. "And no matter what, just smile. I'll hold onto you, so there's nothing to worry about. You'll be fine."

A look of panic leapt into Lee's eyes, and Roddy squeezed her hand again. Her first public appearance with him was rather a big moment, but he believed she would handle it with aplomb, just like everything else.

She obediently took the glasses from Roddy and slipped them over her eyes about a second before their chauffeur opened the door. A thousand flashes seemed to go off the second her feet hit the pavement. The crowd started cheering and chanting the moment Roddy stepped out behind her to take her elbow.

"Smile!" he whispered in her ear, and he couldn't help but grin when she immediately did so, looking as gorgeous as ever.

He led her through the throng, stopping every few feet to sign autographs and banter with his fans. Lee was greedily assessed by dozens of pairs of male eyes, he noted, while the women present wore obvious envy. Lee smiled graciously at them all, and gave the appearance she had been on red carpets dozens of times.

"Who's the lady?" an avid young reporter asked Roddy as he shoved a microphone under his nose.

Roddy felt like punching him, but he smiled instead and put his arm around Lee's waist. "This is Lee."

Inexperienced, Lee made the mistake of lifting her glasses for a moment, and was instantly blinded by camera flashes. She dropped them back down and gripped Roddy's arm like a lifesaver in a stormy sea, but he noted she kept smiling the entire time.

He hurried her inside, filled with admiration. "You're a pro at this."

"I think I'm blind."

"Don't worry, it'll wear off and you'll be able to see just fine in a couple minutes."

Once Lee recuperated, Roddy allowed an usher to lead them to their seats. Lee seemed to enjoy both the movie and his video, though she made a couple comments on the lack of clothes worn by the dancer in the video.

After the movie, Roddy took her to a party in Beverly Hills. Half the population of Los Angeles seemed to be in attendance. The house was packed wall-to-wall with people, and everyone there seemed to know Roddy and want to say hello.

"How do you get through nights like this in one piece?" Lee asked in a rare quiet moment.

"Champagne," he said, grabbing a bottle off a passing waiter's tray.

Once Lee caught a bit of a buzz, she lost a lot of her inhibitions, and she relaxed and seemed to start having fun. Roddy enjoyed the easy way she managed to mingle with the cream of the entertainment world. She treated them like ordinary people, and they all apparently warmed to her. She was unaware of the politics simmering under the surface at the party, and since he didn't give a damn about them, Roddy was amused.

Lee was not in awe of anyone, which could be a dangerous state of affairs in Hollywood, where mountains competed with egos for space. Lee's compliments were genuine, and she just happened to take to all the right people, especially a shy studio head's wife who appreciated her irreverent humor.

"Do you know any of these people?" Lee casually asked her with a wave at the crowd.

The woman gave her a warm smile. "Actually, no."

"Me either," Lee whispered in her ear. "This is my first Hollywood party."

The woman took an instant liking to Lee, and she told Roddy he needed to let Lee get out more so she could make the right acquaintances.

"It would be nice to have some friends," Lee said with sincerity and complete disinterest in Hollywood social climbing, which further endeared her to the woman.

Later, Roddy told Lee, "You have no idea how many people try to get close to her. If you decide you want to be an actress, you're in."

"I'm fine just the way I am," she said firmly, which gave Roddy a warm rush. She certainly was.

They were some of the first guests to leave the party. Roddy had been waiting all day to be alone with Lee, and he was tired of having to share her with the world. All he wanted was to get her home and slowly peel that yellow dress off her, like a banana. Then, he could take his time and savor every delectable inch of her.

"I hope I didn't make a fool of myself tonight," Lee remarked in the limousine on the way home. She kicked off her shoes and wriggled her toes.

"Far from it," Roddy told her as he picked up her

foot and began to rub it.

"Oh, that feels good," she murmured as her eyes slid closed. "I hope nobody remembers me."

Roddy chuckled. "Don't count on it. That dress is going down in history."

Once home, they went directly to the back patio, where Lee melted into Roddy's arms and pressed herself against him before she pulled his head down to hers.

"I've been waiting all day to be alone with you," she murmured against his lips.

"You too?" he said on a groan. "Just feel this." He guided her hand to the bulge in his pants, and she rubbed it slowly over the snakeskin before taking a tug on the laces holding the pants closed.

"I wonder how many snakes it takes to make a pair of these," she wondered.

"Probably just one giant anaconda," Roddy said with disinterest.

"I think it's still alive."

଼

"She stole my press!" Eddie complained.

Roddy laughed and glanced again at the full-color photo of him and Lee smiling into the camera outside the premiere. As expected, Lee had captured the headlines as Roddy's "mystery woman." Somehow, an enterprising reporter had managed to dig up a story about her that was remarkably close to the truth.

"If you went out with a decent woman you wouldn't have anything to worry about," Roddy admonished. "All your Bambis have got to go."

"Listen to you crow," Eddie said on a sneer. "I

can remember a time not so very long ago when your girlfriends could have failed an IQ test."

"That's all in the past. I've moved up in the world."

Roddy felt pretty good about himself that day. The night with Lee had only just begun when they got back from the party the night before. Now, in addition to being responsible for his domestic bliss, Lee had run away with Hollywood's fickle heart. He was infinitely proud of her, coupled with all those other warm, squishy feelings he wasn't ready to analyze. Later would be soon enough to think about those things. For now, he wanted to simply enjoy being led around by a certain part of his anatomy. He wasn't ready to think about how his heart was falling in line the same way. At the moment, all he wanted to do was bask in happiness without worrying about the future.

As usual, just when he thought he might be able to compartmentalize his feelings for her, she appeared. She looked like a cool spring breeze under the hot California sun with her hair hanging loosely down her back and wearing a gauzy, white dress that blew softly around her of its own accord.

"How does it feel to be famous?" was Eddie's greeting.

"Scary," she admitted honestly. "I haven't done anything."

The phone rang as Lee sat down beside Roddy on his chaise, and he answered it with a brusque, "Yeah."

"Why can't you use the manners I tried so hard to teach you when you answer the phone?" Margaret

O'Neill's voice came over the line.

"Hi, Ma," Roddy greeted her without enthusiasm.

"And," she went on sternly, "how is it I have to read about my son's fiancée in the morning paper, and I haven't even met her yet?"

She's not my fiancée! Roddy would have bellowed if Lee had not been sitting right there. Instead, he said, "Gee, Ma, I just got up."

"How long has she been there?"

Roddy gave a guilty shrug. "About three weeks."

"Three weeks, and you haven't said a word about her!"

"I've been busy."

Margaret barked out a laugh. "I'll just bet you have. When are you going to let her out of bed long enough to come out and have lunch with me?"

Roddy cast an anxious glance at Lee. His mother wanted to have lunch with her now? He could just imagine the conversation they would have. Margaret was bound to fall in love with Lee on sight, and then Roddy was sure she would insist he put a ring on her finger. Lee probably wouldn't know how to react to that, and to his way of thinking, she should be spared the discomfort.

What he didn't want to admit was that he really wanted to spare *himself* the discomfort. Deep down, he knew Lee would have no problems handling herself in any situation, particularly after last night. What Roddy really wanted to protect was his own personal freedom.

"Soon, Ma," he hedged.

"How about tomorrow?" Margaret pushed, not

about to be put off. "This article says you're hard at work in the studio, and it also says she quit her job for you, so I'm sure she's dying of boredom locked away at your house. She's probably starved for female companionship."

Margaret's reproach could not be ignored. She didn't like being left out of anything, and she wasn't going to give up until Roddy gave in.

"I'll talk to her, okay, Ma?" he promised, having no intention of doing it for at least a few more days.

"Great!" his mother said with enthusiasm. "I'll be there tomorrow at noon to pick her up." She hung up before he could argue.

Roddy set the phone down feeling like a doomed man.

"That was my mother," he said to Lee and Eddie's curious looks. "She wants to have lunch with Lee tomorrow."

"Oh." Lee looked a little nervous. "Of course I want to meet your mother. I'll ask Rosa to make us something special."

Roddy groaned on the inside. He could already imagine the next conversation he would have with his mother. She would gush on and on about how much fun she had dining by the pool with Lee, and she would be sure to tell him what a lovely young woman Lee was, with asides about how well she had obviously taken to living in Roddy's house, which had been in dire need of a woman's touch before. Then she would start in again on how he should marry her.

Roddy stole a glance at Eddie, who seemed inordinately amused by it all. He knew Margaret almost as well as Roddy did, and he was probably already making plans to hang out at Roddy's house as much as possible for a front row seat. Eddie was having way too much fun at his expense since Roddy met Lee.

He gave Roddy an insincere smile. "Too bad we have to be at the studio all day tomorrow, huh, Rod?"

"Yeah."

Roddy's fingers played lightly over Lee's arm and he kept a smile on his face for her benefit, but his mind was in turmoil.

CHAPTER THIRTEEN

Beginning with lunch with Margaret O'Neill, Lee's life developed a sort of pattern. She and Margaret hit it off, and started dining together often. Sometimes it was at Roddy's house, and at others in various restaurants in the Los Angeles area. Other days, Lee went out shopping, or to exercise classes with the various girlfriends of Eddie and the other members of the band. When she was alone, which was often, she liked to lie by the pool with music blaring, or if she was bored, she took her new car out for drives.

Lee had settled on something reasonable, a Miata convertible in bright yellow with black trim. She liked her car and made heads turn as she zoomed down the freeway with her hair in the wind.

Since the day of the movie premiere when Roddy hadn't found Lee at home, he had also provided her with a cell phone. Though she voiced the usual objections, he could tell she liked the slim little device. He liked the fact that he could talk to her any time he wanted now that she had it, and he called her several times a day. It hadn't taken long for her to start calling him, too, since he was always thrilled to hear her voice.

Roddy's life had never been better. His days at the studio were going extremely well, and everything for the new disk seemed to be coming together with ease. The guys even seemed to be better musicians, if that was possible, and Roddy's voice was in rare form. The executives at his record company were already rubbing their hands together in anticipation of another platinum hit.

Roddy was encouraged to get as much exposure as possible. After Lee's Hollywood debut, they even decided she was good for his image, and were attempting to arrange a photo session for the two of them. So far, Roddy had refused to cooperate and hadn't bothered to tell Lee about it. The whole world knew he and Lee were a couple, but the thought of them posing together in his house seemed too intrusive.

Rather than agree to photo sessions with Lee, Roddy took her out in public a lot. She had already filled her half of their closet with an array of leather, velvet, silk, and denim, complete with shoes in every shape and style to match. It amused Roddy that photographers loved her and she always got into snapshots with him. Their pictures were published by the dozen in pulpy fan magazines filled with gossip about musicians and their lifestyles. Roddy often did interviews for such magazines, but he refused all requests to have Lee present for them, and refused to answer any questions about her.

One night, Roddy's band got together with a few other bands who were going to appear together on a television special. Everyone brought their wives and girlfriends, and Lee was surprised to find out for the first time that Mike was actually married. She always saw him at parties with different young women, and she told Roddy it had never occurred to her he might have a wife hidden away somewhere. She was even more stunned when she saw how beautiful Mike's wife was, and found out they had children.

Roddy could tell she was disgusted by the state of affairs. He already knew she didn't really approve of Eddie and the way he ended his relationship with Claire. Roddy's explanation that Claire didn't expect fidelity and she only cared about his money didn't excuse Eddie, in Lee's opinion. Lee was even more disgusted with Mike because it was obvious his wife was very much in love with him, and seemed clueless about his rather constant affairs. She expressed amazement that Mike managed to keep it secret.

After conveying her opinions about the morals of his band members, Lee got quiet on the way home, and Roddy found himself perturbed.

"You haven't said much," he said as they sat by the pool once they got home. "Is something wrong?"

"I was just wondering how a man can have a wonderful wife at home and still want to run around with other women," Lee said softly.

Roddy knew he should tread carefully, or not at all, but he heard himself ask, "What do you mean?"

"Like Mike," she said, turning to look at him. "His wife couldn't be more beautiful, and they've got three kids, but I see him all the time with other girls."

Roddy shrugged and relaxed just a bit. "I guess that's just the kind of guy Mike is."

"I wonder why guys like that bother to get married at all," Lee went on. "He can't keep his affairs secret forever, and when she finds out, all hell is going to break loose."

"Maybe Mike had good intentions at first," Roddy mused. "Maybe he thought he was ready to settle down, but it didn't last. It can happen with all the willing women out there."

"Maybe that will happen with you."

Roddy hoped she didn't hear his sharply indrawn breath. "I'm not married."

"No," she agreed slowly, her voice dropping in pitch, "but you do have a commitment of sorts with me. I wonder sometimes when you'll change your mind about it."

Roddy immediately went on the defensive. "Where did this come from?" he heard himself snarl, shooting to his feet and pacing a few steps before turning to glare at a startled Lee. "Have I done anything to make you not trust me? Don't I take you out? Why are you suddenly doubting me because of someone else's actions?"

"Roddy! I—"

He cut her off. "Whatever, Lee. I knew you'd start in on me one of these days, and right now I just don't want to hear it!"

He turned on his heel and stomped back into the house. He grabbed his keys on his way through and went right out the front, then squealed away in his Maserati a few seconds later.

ଔ

Lee sat stunned on a lounger by the pool. She had not expected Roddy's rather intense reaction to her mildly-voiced statement.

Her first impulse was to go after him and apologize for insinuating their relationship lacked permanence. Honestly, Roddy had given her no reason to doubt him, and she had no basis for making accusations. When she thought about it, though, Lee knew she had not made any outrageous accusations, and Roddy had overreacted.

Though she carefully did not dwell on them, Lee knew there were reasons behind Roddy's erratic behavior that night. She had touched a sore spot when she questioned his level of commitment to her. Though nobody mentioned it, the whole world knew she was there with him on borrowed time. One day, Roddy would tire of her, and they would be through. The only promise he had made was that there would be no other women while they were together. The future had not been discussed.

It was out there, though, and Lee knew that at some point she would have to give it some consideration. The moment Roddy's eyes began to roam, she would be gone. She would not wait around for him to ask her to leave, and she certainly didn't want a payoff when the time came. That such a time would come was an absolute certainty; Lee simply did not know when it would be.

Despite all of that, making the decision to stay with Roddy had been easy. She exchanged the life of a working single girl to become the pampered girlfriend of a rock star. The transition was not a difficult one to make, and the first few weeks had been a whirlwind of exciting new things. Now that she had become accustomed to her new existence, Lee found she liked it quite a bit. The only thing not to like was the impermanence.

Though she was afraid to tell him, Lee wanted it all. She was more in love with Roddy than a woman had a right to be. Every time the phone rang during the day, she leapt for it, anticipating his call. She looked forward to him returning home every afternoon, and reveled in the time they spent together. Everything was perfect when it was just the two of them, and she had honestly never had more fun than when Roddy took her out in public. Naturally, she didn't want it to end. She wanted to take it a step further, and really build a life together. Lee didn't know how Roddy would feel if she said any of those things, though, so she kept them to herself.

He cared for her and enjoyed having her in his house. It wasn't enough, but for now it would just have to do.

☙

Somehow, Roddy managed to avoid getting a ticket that night. He drove out to the coast road and recklessly raced along its curves until he got his emotions under control. Even as he slammed out of the house, he knew he wasn't really angry with Lee. She had simply brought up a sore subject. Since she moved into his house, it seemed the entire world was demanding he commit himself to her. She was actually the only one who didn't push.

Lee's comments hadn't just come out of left field, he knew. Roddy was aware that a snazzy car and a credit card to shop with were hardly the signs of a lasting commitment. She had plenty of reasons to question his intentions. When she moved in, she gave up her source of income, as well as her own home. Lee's future was unclear, even to Roddy, but despite the guilt that assailed him, he wasn't ready to offer her more. The very thought of making a real commitment made him break out in a cold sweat.

If he wanted to be honest with himself, Roddy knew he had a number of things to feel guilty about. He felt bad that he couldn't spend more time with Lee, and that she was uncertain about her future. At the moment, though, he mostly just felt like a jerk for flipping out on her and stomping out of the house just because she had the nerve to question him.

His feelings of remorse were rather foreign territory. Roddy usually didn't care enough about other people's feelings to take them into consideration. He just didn't give a damn if it didn't directly affect him, and if someone got mad, that was their problem. He was Roddy O'Neill, and he lived life by his own rules. So why was this fight with Lee eating him up?

Unable to answer the question, Roddy simply turned his car around and raced for home.

The house was dark when he got there, and he tiptoed upstairs to look for Lee. Fear assailed him when he found his bed empty and untouched. It hadn't occurred to him while he was out driving around that Lee might have up and left. Now, however, he was faced with an empty bedroom, and not so much as a lipsticked note on the bathroom mirror.

Roddy quickly searched the entire house, and then, with his heart in his throat, he let himself out to the back patio. If he hadn't been searching, he might not have found Lee, who was curled up asleep on a deck chair. Warmth suffused his entire body when he spotted her, just before he was overtaken by feelings of guilt. It struck him that she was still on the patio because she might have been unwilling to sleep in their bed. He didn't like the way that made him feel at all.

He just stared at her for several minutes. She looked like a fallen angel who had broken a wing. Her soft lips were gently parted in sleep, and her hands were curled over her chest. She was still dressed in a now-rumpled skirt and blouse which helped her blend into the shadows.

Going with instinct, Roddy dropped down on his haunches to kiss her lips. As he did, her eyes opened to stare into his. What he saw there caused little arrows to pierce his heart. Of their own accord, his arms reached out to enfold her against him, and before he realized it had happened, their bodies were entwined on the chaise.

"I'm sorry," they said in unison against each other's lips.

"It's not your fault Mike is the way he is," Lee said quietly. "I shouldn't compare you to him."

Roddy sighed long and slow. "It's my fault, Lee. You have a right to wonder about the future. I haven't exactly promised you a lot because I can't. I'm not going to lie to you or make promises I can't keep. But I keep the promises I make."

She nodded. "I know."

He stroked her hair and indicated the house and grounds with a sweeping arm gesture. "Don't ever think I don't want you here," he went on. "This is your home."

She gave him a slight smile and said, "Okay."

With relief that the crisis had passed, Roddy decided to get back on comfortable ground, and he pressed his hips suggestively against hers. "Why don't we go upstairs and I'll show you why I don't want any other woman?"

If Lee wanted to argue, he gave her no chance. He lunged to his feet and pulled her into his arms. For the second time, Roddy played Rhett Butler and carried her up the curving staircase to his bedroom. Once there, he cast all courtly pretenses aside and tore her clothes off her body and carelessly flung them over his shoulder. The only thing that mattered at that moment was feeling his skin on hers, and he lost himself in the flurry of their passion.

❧

Lee gazed though half-lidded eyes at Roddy as he slept in the darkness. Things were back to normal between them, and everything was okay now. Or was it? Everything was normal again, at least. Though she didn't know how long it would last, she still had a place in Roddy's life. The future was out there, but it was unwise to think about it too much. It was better to think only about the glorious present and enjoy life moment by moment.

She stared at their tangled limbs with a smile. It looked as if elves had come in the night and tied the sheets in knots while she and Roddy slept. She tugged her foot and found herself jammed. Apparently, they would need a scissors, or at least a Boy Scout handbook, in order to get out of bed.

She felt Roddy's leg twitch. "I can't move," he said, startling her out of her thoughts. He kicked at the sheets again and grunted when he was still stuck fast.

Lee struggled to move a leg and found herself just as stuck. "I can't move, either."

"Maybe I can reach the phone and dial 911," Roddy suggested lightly.

Lee had to laugh. "I can just see the headline. 'Rock star and girlfriend rescued from clutches of hungry bed!'"

Roddy laughed along with her. "I'm afraid of what our rescuers would have to say." He tugged at the sheets again. "Now that I'm stuck, I'm getting hungry."

Lee ran a hand down his chest. "You know," she murmured against his skin, "maybe we should try getting out of this the same way we got in."

Roddy ceased his struggles and she felt his hand on her thigh. "You mean, do this?"

"Yes."

"And maybe this?"

They forgot about their predicament and anything else for quite some time.

The next morning found Roddy and Lee miraculously free from the sheets, and Roddy was able to get up and go to work as usual. That day, the band was beginning work on a new video, which was sure to keep Roddy very busy. He would be working longer hours than usual for the next few weeks, and Lee would have to find a way to fill them.

It was getting harder and harder to stave off the boredom. At first, with the newness of her surroundings, Lee kept herself busy sightseeing and acclimating herself to her new home. By now, she had to admit she was bored stiff. She could only sit in the sun for so many hours, and there was really only so much shopping a girl could do. Roddy had yet to complain about the bills, but she still felt guilty. Lee supposed she could draw her own map of the Los Angeles basin from the hundreds of miles she had put on her car driving aimlessly around it. She went to lunch with people she barely knew and took tennis lessons, even though she wasn't all that fond of tennis.

It was easy to forget how mundane her days were when Roddy came home at night, though. When they were together, she forgot everything else and simply basked in her happiness. Nothing seemed all that bad when he held her in his arms. In fact, everything seemed worth it when they were together.

That the perfect little bubble popped every morning when Roddy left was something Lee knew she couldn't hold off facing forever. That day in particular, the loneliness and boredom were particularly crushing, and it made her start to think.

She had to find a purpose in life, aside from loving Roddy O'Neill. Lee was afraid to divulge the depth of her feelings to him, especially after last night, but she could admit them to herself. What she did not want to think about was that it might not be enough to keep them together. She was not really happy living in his shadow, and needed something of her own to strive for. Several ideas were examined and rejected, and in the end, Lee decided to go shopping again and worry about it tomorrow. Sometimes, it was better not to upset the apple cart, and since Roddy had stomped out on her the night before, this was definitely one of those times.

CHAPTER FOURTEEN

Lee's life soon became as monotonous as the television schedule she followed. She slept as late as possible every day to shorten the hours between the time she awoke and the time Roddy came home. When she awakened, it was to reach immediately for the remote control to watch a few hours of brainless game shows and sitcom reruns. Once she grew bored with inactivity, Lee would roll out of bed to don one of her many colorful swimsuits and then spend several hours swimming laps or lying by the pool. By the time that began to wear thin, Lee went back into the house to change clothes, no longer taking note of the beauty of Roddy's marble staircase or the old world art he collected. Dressed in a daytime outfit of painted-on jeans and a tee-shirt, Lee then headed out to drive around LA. A couple times a week, she broke up the routine by having lunch or shopping with one of her new friends, but most of her time was spent in solitude.

Everything changed the moment Roddy came home every day. He always looked so good to her, and she enjoyed the way the weariness seemed to seep out of him whenever they laid eyes on each other.

His hair was usually a mess from the number of times he ran his hands through it, and his jeans were always creased and smudged, but no matter what, he always looked wonderful.

Roddy enjoyed hanging out at home with Lee, but he also liked to take her out. She had been on his arm at some of the hottest LA nightclubs, where their picture never failed to be snapped at least once. He also took her to movie premieres, Hollywood parties, and other dizzying social events.

And yet, Lee felt more and more restless by the day. No matter how much fun she and Roddy had together, all the hours she spent alone threatened to cave in on her.

One afternoon, while lying idly by the pool, she decided she'd had enough. She simply was not cut out to do nothing. She needed something to do, a goal to reach for, a reason to get out of bed every day. Some ideas had occurred to her that she wanted to discuss with Roddy, but Lee was not yet ready to make sweeping changes that might undermine what little security she had. Instead, she decided to start with something small and work her way up.

She had made one real friend in Los Angeles, and Lee decided to call her and see if she could find a partner in crime. Helene was the girlfriend of the lead guitarist of a popular LA band called Street Trash. Helene, or Hell, as she was called most often, was close to Lee's age and seemed to have a working brain in her head, so it was natural she and Lee developed a friendship. Lee realized Helene might not like her idea, but then again, it was just silly and off-the-wall enough that she might love it.

"Hey, Lee! Glad you called," Helene enthusiastically answered her phone. "I was thinking about checking out a new shop on Melrose and thought you might want to come along."

"Sure, and I've got another idea, too." Lee's tone was conspiratorial.

Helene couldn't resist it. "Okay. Forget the shopping. Your idea sounds better already. What is it?"

"Let's take guitar lessons," Lee suggested.

"Guitar lessons!" Helene shrieked, only to be quickly hushed.

"I want to keep it a secret," Lee suggested. "By this time, I think I've read every book ever published and I need something besides shopping to keep me busy. I might as well learn a new skill."

"Bored, huh?"

Lee sighed. "Yeah."

"Why don't you join the health club with me? There are lots of bored people there, and…"

"I just dropped a membership, Helene. I was taking tennis lessons, and I was so bad it was just a waste of money. Besides, I'm not into the whole clubby social climbing and backstabbing thing."

"Probably the main reason you'll never really be a success in this town," Helene joked. She got a huge kick out of social climbing and backstabbing, proclaiming it better than television.

"So," Lee pushed, "are you up for guitar lessons or not? I can go by myself, but I thought it would be more fun to do it with a friend."

"Isn't everything?" Helene gave a quick laugh. "Of course I'm up for it. I can't let you become the next big musician without me."

From that day forward, Lee and Helene took guitar lessons twice a week. To her surprise, Lee was not quickly bored with it, as she was with everything else she tried. To her amazement, she actually had some aptitude and was having fun with her lessons. Even when Helene dropped out after a few weeks, Lee kept at it.

Her new hobby wasn't really enough to pull her out of her rut, but at least Lee wasn't lying in bed for hours every morning watching mindless television. Learning the guitar alleviated her boredom somewhat, though she still felt pangs of loneliness. She hoped those would go away as she opened up new parts of her life, and had a vision in her head of one day being able to jam with Roddy when she was good enough. He still sang for her sometimes when he wanted her to hear a new song he was working on, and she hoped he would be pleased that they could do even more together now that she was learning the guitar.

For the time being, though, she kept her lessons a secret. She wasn't very confident in her abilities yet, and wanted to stay quiet until she was a bit more skilled. Lee knew she would never attain Eddie's level of expertise, because few did, but she wanted to at least be competent. It was easy to indulge her new hobby with the old guitars Roddy left lying around the house. Lee borrowed one for her lessons and practice, and simply made sure she was done and the guitar put back where she found it before he came home at night.

⚘

Roddy was in a foul mood. Nothing had gone right that day. It was the day they were supposed to start filming the new video, but fate had decided otherwise. Not one, but three lights had blown within the first fifteen minutes of the shoot. Then, one of the amps refused to work and they had to wait an hour for a suitable replacement. When they were all ready to start filming again, Roddy couldn't find the right bandanna and refused to use a substitute. They wasted more time while three production assistants searched high and low for it, finally finding it at the bottom of a pile of other bandannas. The rest of the band was thoroughly irritated with Roddy by then, but he didn't care. He was a perfectionist, and everything had to be just right.

When the details finally fell into place, it suddenly got worse again. Tempers were already high when the dancer who had been chosen by the record company came prancing out onto the set. It was someone else's job to cast dancers and Roddy had never seen her before, so he lost it when she appeared looking like Lee's evil twin. Her hair had been dyed to the exact same shade as Lee's, and it was teased all over her head to fall into a sea of disorganized curls down her back. Her makeup was overdone and her dress would have fit on a Barbie doll.

Roddy had been talking to Mike about a couple fine points, but he stopped mid-phrase and threw a clipboard at the smiling record company executive who was foolhardy enough to be on the set that day.

"What the hell is this?" he bellowed at the shocked man.

"It—it's your dancer," the nervous executive stammered after the clipboard barely missed his head.

"Whose idea was she?" Roddy raged. "She looks almost exactly like my girlfriend!"

"She's supposed to," the guy in the suit explained. "We thought—"

"Oh, no she's not!" Roddy clenched his fists and took a couple of steps toward the unfortunate man. "When did I ask for a dancer who looks like my girlfriend on crack?"

"Hey!" the dancer protested, only to be ignored.

"We thought since your girlfriend appears in so many photos with you that it would be good for the video." The executive wore an earnest expression but looked ready to run away.

"See how good it is for the video when I'm not in it!" Roddy snarled. "I'm not having this bimbo in my video. She looks like Lee turning tricks."

"Hey!" the dancer piped up again, this time drawing Roddy's attention.

"Sorry, sweetie," he told her, "but somebody made a mistake and you've got to go."

"I've got a contract!" she argued.

"Bully for you. Use it to get into someone else's video," Roddy muttered, already bored with the situation. "You're not going to be in mine."

He turned and stomped off to his trailer. He knew he would get his way and the new dancer would not only not look exactly like Lee, she would bear no resemblance to his girlfriend whatsoever. The record company would probably provide a brunette with blue eyes and a voluptuous figure.

An hour later, Eddie knocked on his door. Eddie was the only one who dared approach him by then.

"They got a new girl," he announced when he poked his head in.

"And?"

"She'll pass inspection. Brown hair, blue eyes, different build, the works."

Roddy smiled. He knew his record company as well as they knew him. "Would you mind telling me how we wound up with the other girl?"

"You never show up for the auditions," Eddie said with a shrug, "and the rest of us thought you might like her, so she was hired."

"You thought I'd like her? Are you crazy?"

"We screwed up. It happens every now and then."

"I guess. Are we still doing the shoot today?"

Eddie laughed. "Unless you want to give another suit-and-tie guy a heart attack, yes, we're still shooting today."

Roddy had calmed down since his outburst, but he was still in no mood to be placid and reasonable. He snapped at everybody and reduced the new dancer to tears twice when she made mistakes, but they got the video shot.

When the interminable day was finally over, Roddy went back to his trailer to change out of his costume and back into his everyday clothes, which weren't all that much different. He waved goodbye to his grateful band members and made a beeline for his car, glad to leave the video set behind and get back home to his sweet, sane Lee.

It still wasn't his day. Halfway home, his favorite Led Zeppelin CD started skipping, and he wound up flinging it out the window in frustration when he couldn't get it to work right. When he stomped on the gas in frustration, he picked up a tail, and got a speeding ticket on top of everything else. The cop was unimpressed with who he was, and Roddy was in a rare mood by the time he finally got home.

ଔ

Lee hoped Roddy remembered they were supposed to be present at the grand opening of a record store that evening. She had already been dressed for an hour, and still there was no sign of him. She knew the band was filming a video that day, and that filming was an unpredictable process, so rather than worrying she decided to simply relax and kill the time.

It was a good opportunity to practice a new song she had been learning on the guitar. She was very close to letting Roddy in on her secret hobby, so she had been practicing twice as much as usual over the last few days in an effort to impress him. She took the guitar that was usually leaning up against their bedroom wall and sat by a chair in front of the window to immerse herself in the music she was so certain would bring them closer together, and waited for Roddy to come home.

CHAPTER FIFTEEN

Roddy trudged up the steps, his booted feet silent on the thick carpet runner. Now that he was home and much calmer, he felt worn out. He needed a nice, hot shower and a long nap, but as luck would have it, he was supposed to open a record store that evening. At the moment, he would have fired someone over it if he could, but knew he had only himself to blame.

Thank God he had Lee to keep him sane, he thought as a smile began to play at the corners of his mouth. She always knew just how to make him feel better, even on days like this when his schedule seemed to stretch on forever.

He stopped when he heard noise coming from his bedroom. It sounded like an acoustic guitar. He wondered if Eddie had beaten him home and was out by the pool, with the sound drifting in through the windows. But that wasn't likely since he knew Eddie had other plans that night. Besides, whoever was playing the guitar lacked Eddie's practiced skill. Curious, as well as perturbed, Roddy silently advanced on his bedroom door and, with a shove, sent it crashing against the wall, hoping to startle the guitar player.

It worked. Lee nearly jumped out of her skin and almost dropped the guitar.

Roddy froze in his tracks. Of all the scenarios he had imagined, he hadn't thought he would find Lee playing the guitar. He didn't even know she could play.

"What's going on in here?" he asked sharply.

Lee swallowed and looked at a loss for words for a moment, then said, "I was playing the guitar."

"Obviously." It was said on a sneer.

Lee's brow furrowed and she carefully set the instrument on the floor next to her chair.

Roddy advanced a step. "I didn't know you could play." This was an accusation.

"I started taking lessons awhile ago," she explained softly.

He kicked the door shut and advanced on her, his temper slipping again. "You *what?* Why?"

"I needed something to do," was her simple answer. Her posture was defensive and she stared him right in the eye. "I wanted to learn the guitar so I could—"

"So you could start your own little band and get your picture in the paper without me?" he cut her off in a voice laced with derision.

For a moment, she simply stared at him in open-mouthed disbelief. Then she visibly lost her temper and advanced on him.

"Why shouldn't I?" she spat, venom in every word. "Are you the only one who's allowed a career around here? Am I supposed to spend the rest of my life shopping and waiting for you to show up?"

Her words hit home, so he responded with angry bluster. "I see. I guess I've been pretty convenient for you all this time. Being linked with my name was just your first step."

She snorted and let loose an ugly laugh. "My name isn't linked with yours, Roddy. You don't make commitments, remember?"

"Maybe I just don't make them with users," he heard himself say, even knowing full well it wasn't a fair accusation. Lee didn't give a damn about his money or fame, but he had to lash out at her somehow.

Lee reached him in three long strides, fire and brimstone in her eyes. "Explain to me how I've used you, Roddy."

A tiny voice in his brain screamed at him to shut up, but he ignored it. Instead, his arm swept the room in a broad gesture.

"Explain to me how you're not," he countered. "How much stuff did you bring with you when you came? A suitcase? You didn't even have a car when I met you."

Hurt leapt into her eyes before they narrowed to slits. "You bastard. I didn't ask you for anything. I didn't *want* anything! You made me take it!"

He looked away and ran a hand through his hair before turning to regard her again. "It sure didn't seem like it was all that hard for you, Lee. You sure adjusted fast."

Roddy was used to tears and wailing from women, but the angrier she got, the more quiet Lee became.

"Yes, I did." Her voice was so soft he barely

heard her. "Because being with you was important to me. I didn't have much when I met you, Roddy, but it was all mine. And I gave it up for you."

His smile was snide. "Such a sacrifice. I guess I should be grateful."

Lee never did anything like other women, and that day was no exception. Her mouth worked for a second, and then she gave up on the argument and just punched him in the jaw. She hit him so hard he nearly went down. He stood there and rubbed his face in disbelief while she held him immobile with a stony glare.

"I don't know what happened to you today, and I don't care," she hissed through her teeth. "Because from this moment forward, I'm going to start caring about *me* again. I need a life and living in your shadow isn't it! You think it's okay that you're out living your dreams while I sit and wait for you, but I've got news for you, Roddy. It isn't. I'm so bored I'm losing my mind, and I haven't stuck it out for shopping I don't care about or a stupid car. I stayed here because I love you."

Her bottom lip quivered and she turned and grabbed her purse off the floor before stomping out the door and slamming it shut behind her.

"I love you, too," Roddy finally admitted, but it was too late. She was already on the other side of the door.

He ran a hand over his sore jaw again and shook his head at his own stupidity. He wasn't sure what had gotten into him, or why he had said the terrible, hurtful things that passed his lips. He didn't mean any of them. If he wanted to really think about it, he knew he had done it because he was scared of her and the power she held over him. He was frightened of the way she made him feel. He knew what he offered her was not enough, but was terrified to open his heart and give her more.

How could he ever have thought it would last? Why would it when he couldn't even make her any promises? He knew if his money really mattered to her, that would have been enough, but it wasn't. Fame wasn't part of her program, either. She had made a number of important contacts around LA, but she didn't make use of any of them. She only wanted to be with him, and he knew it.

Now that she had stormed away, he suddenly looked at their relationship from a new perspective. Maybe opening his heart a little more wouldn't kill him. Truthfully, though he hadn't been willing to admit it even to himself, she already owned his heart. He just couldn't let her know.

He wondered why it was so hard to admit he loved her, even to himself, and didn't like the answers. He was a rock star, and women threw themselves at him. Falling in love with one woman and making a commitment to her would mean giving up his special status and acting like a regular guy, and Roddy O'Neill held himself above that.

What a moron.

Almost too late, he realized just how foolish he was. None of the hundreds of women who had visited his dressing room meant a thing, but Lee was his salvation. He realized how bored and dissatisfied he had been with everything until she came along, and then he just took her for granted.

Well, it wasn't too late. He would go after her and tell her he loved her, and even offer her a future. It made him grit his teeth, but he vowed he would even help her start a music career if that was what she wanted. Whatever made her happy was worth it.

He strode over to the bedroom door and flung it open, but the house was quiet.

"Lee!" he yelled.

The house sounded even quieter after his outburst. Scowling, Roddy left the bedroom and quickly searched every room on the second floor, but all were empty. His perusal of the first floor had the same result. By the time he went outside to check the back yard, his heart was slamming against his ribs. Lee wasn't there. He felt a glimmer of hope when he remembered to check the garage, but became alarmed again when he found her car there, yet no sign of Lee.

Roddy slumped and dragged his feet as he went back to the house. He went straight to the game room and poured a stiff drink before picking up the phone to dial Eddie.

"Eddie!" Roddy howled when Eddie picked up.

"Roddy? What's wrong? Are you in jail?" Eddie was immediately concerned.

"I'm home. It's Lee."

"What's wrong? Is she okay?"

"She left."

"For good?" Eddie was tactless enough to act.

A shard of alarm pierced Roddy's heart. "God, I hope not. I flipped out on her when I got home and she took off."

Eddie sighed. "It had to happen sooner or later. I can't believe you didn't mess it up before this. That woman doesn't take crap from anybody."

"Yeah, well I'm glad you're so impressed," Roddy grumbled. "This is serious. I said some nasty stuff and she even hit me before she left."

"She slapped you?" Eddie was incredulous. Obviously, he cared more about the juicy details than Roddy's predicament.

"She punched me," Roddy corrected, rubbing his jaw again. The woman had a mean right hook.

"She *punched* you?" Eddie erupted into gales of laughter. "Oh, man, I'd have paid to see that!"

Roddy waited patiently for Eddie's laughter to subside. "I gotta find her, Eddie," he said in a pathetically small voice.

Eddie sobered instantly. "Yeah, but don't you have an opening somewhere tonight?"

Roddy turned the air blue. He had forgotten his commitment.

"I'll come and get you," Eddie said on a sigh. "You can't not go. I'll call Helene and ask her to wait at your house until Lee gets there. They can talk trash about you until we get back."

"Who's Helene?" Roddy wondered, suddenly feeling like a heel for not knowing. Apparently, there was a lot about Lee he had ignored.

Eddie's tone was a bit accusatory. "She's Lee's best friend in LA."

"Can't you just do the promo without me so I can wait for Lee?"

"No," Eddie said firmly. "You promised them Roddy O'Neill, and they expect Roddy O'Neill. Unless you want to see stories about your fight in the tabloids tomorrow. You know those reporters are psychic sometimes."

Roddy grumbled about it, but he caved in. "Pick me up and let's get it over with."

"I had other plans tonight, you know."

"Not anymore."

Eddie sighed, but Roddy knew he would be there. Eddie owed him.

ଔ

Roddy looked like hell, in Eddie's opinion. He supposed it stood to reason, after Roddy knocked back half a bottle of scotch. His pants were fine but his shirt looked slept in, his eyes were bloodshot, and his hair was a mess.

Feeling like Roddy's mother, Eddie ushered him upstairs to change his shirt, comb his hair and get a bandanna in place, and find a nice, dark pair of sunglasses to hide his eyes. Finally satisfied, he propelled Roddy down to his Mercedes, which had a pouting girl in the backseat.

"Hi!" Roddy greeted her with his scotch breath. "Have you seen a blonde lurking in the bushes?"

She gave him an odd look as Eddie started the car.

"Never mind him," he told his date. "He's had a bad day and a few too many drinks. He's usually almost normal."

The record store opening was tedious, and Eddie gritted his teeth through the whole thing. An absolute mob of girls was in attendance, all screaming,

"We love you!" to both Roddy and Eddie. Roddy seemed even more annoyed than Eddie that his picture was taken more than ever, but Roddy was alone for once, and he looked like hell. That was far more interesting to the gathered paparazzi than everyday, pretty boy Eddie.

After what felt like an eternity, the festivities were over and they could finally leave. Eddie was only too glad to see the last of Roddy, who had been a royal pain in the ass all night long. When he wasn't leering and making loud, inappropriate comments, he moped and stared off into space.

Eddie wasn't sure if it was a good idea to leave Roddy alone when he dropped him off, but he had never been so anxious to get away from his best friend.

~

Helene had her head in the refrigerator when Roddy came into the kitchen.

"Is Lee back yet?" he said in lieu of hello.

A redhead he couldn't remember ever having met turned to glare at him. "No. I haven't seen her. Want to tell me why she left?"

He glared back at her with zero effect. "No, I don't. It's private."

Helene sniffed. "Eddie said you were pretty upset. I'm glad. You must have messed up pretty bad if she left you. You better hope she comes back."

Helene's words were not reassuring, and Roddy gulped.

Her expression softened somewhat as Helene opened a can of soda and took a sip. "Look, I don't want to get in the middle of your business, but maybe I can help. Maybe I can find her and talk to her or something. But it would help if you told me what's going on."

Roddy sank onto a barstool at the kitchen counter and stared at a spot on the wall for several seconds before he spoke again. "I said some really dumb things about her being with me for my money and my stuff."

Helene just laughed. "That's a good one. I shop with her a lot, and she's always talking about how this or that would look good with what you wear. It's always about you with her. She could probably go out and buy herself some jewelry or some other investments for the future, but I don't think her mind works that way."

"I know," he agreed as he ran a hand through his hair for the umpteenth time that day. "I didn't mean any of what I said. I had a bad day that just kept getting worse and worse, and then I came home and found her playing the guitar. I didn't even know she could play."

Helene took another sip from her can. "She just started taking lessons not long ago. She was bored and wanted to find something useful to do, and figured you guys could jam together if she learned the guitar."

"So she's not joining a band?"

The look Helene fixed him with made him feel an inch tall. "Lee in a band? Roddy, you're so stupid."

Apparently, there was more than one woman who wasn't in awe of him, but Roddy was in no mood to appreciate it that night. He just wanted to find Lee and bring her home.

"What's so stupid about that? Everyone in LA has an angle."

"What makes you think Lee would ever want to be in a band?" Helene countered. "She had just barely started getting used to having her picture taken with you. That was all the publicity she needed. She liked being a librarian, you know. And she liked that it made her different from everyone else around here. Besides, if Lee wanted to be in a band, don't you think she would have talked to you about it? Who's more connected than you?"

It all made perfect sense when Roddy thought about it. Actually, the only part of the equation that didn't seem to make sense was him.

"Where would she go?" he asked in some desperation. It worried him greatly that Lee had not yet come home.

"Did you try your mom's?" Helene suggested. "Other than me and you, your mom is the only person she's really gotten close to."

"Really?"

Helene looked disgusted with him again. "Did you expect her to become best friends with the dizbrains Eddie dates?"

"I guess not."

Despite his trepidation, Roddy reached for the phone to dial his mother. It wouldn't matter that the hour was late or that he would be waking her up. She would light into him no matter what because of what he had said to Lee.

There was sleep in Margaret's voice when she murmured a hello, but she woke up fast when Roddy tried to casually ask, "Is Lee over there?"

"What's going on?" Margaret immediately wanted to know. "Why isn't she with you?"

"We had a fight," was Roddy's vague response. He should have known he wouldn't get away with it.

"Must have been some fight if you think she'd come here at midnight." She paused a moment and then added, "What have you done, Roddy?"

Roddy was getting tired of everyone automatically assuming he was the bad guy. "Nothing! We had an argument, which was *private*, and she walked out and hasn't come home. I'm worried about her and thought you might have heard from her."

"No, I haven't. But if I see her, I'll take care of her," Margaret promised.

"Will you also please give me a call so I know she's okay?" Roddy felt it necessary to ask. Judging by his mother's tone, she didn't seem very concerned about his state of mind.

Margaret sighed. "Yes, I'll call you."

The moment Roddy hung up, Helene turned to him. "Is she there?"

"Nope. My mother hasn't seen her."

"Well, I should get home. Max'll worry about me if I don't get back pretty soon. Besides, if Lee comes to my house…"

"Yeah. Thanks, Helene."

Roddy settled down to wait for Lee by himself. His companion was a brand-new bottle of vodka from the bar in his study. He fell asleep by the time it was half empty and awakened to bright sunlight and a shrilling telephone.

He groped for the phone with fingers that refused to obey his commands, and his eyes felt as if they were filled with sand.

"Yeah," he rasped into the receiver.

"Roddy?" It was Margaret. "Is she back yet?"

"Who?"

"Lee!"

Oh, God, Lee. The night before came rushing back, and Roddy slumped on the sofa.

"I don't think so," was all he could say.

"Well, find out and call me back!" Margaret ordered, and then she hung up.

Roddy couldn't remember the last time his head hurt so bad. It banged and throbbed with his every brain wave. Movement proved extremely difficult, and agony lanced through his head when he tried to sit up.

His headache was nothing compared to the pain in his heart, though, especially after Rosa reported that Lee was not on the premises.

Roddy stood and stared at the valley below. Lee was out there somewhere, but where? When was she coming home? She would come home, wouldn't she?

CHAPTER SIXTEEN

Lee was furious, but under that veneer, she was simply hurt and miserable.

She still couldn't believe Roddy had said those things to her. The more she thought, the more she could only come up with one reason for it: he meant them. Somewhere along the line, she had allowed herself to forget that she meant nothing more than any of the other women who had come before her. It didn't matter who or what she was on the inside, because Roddy didn't see it. All he saw was yet another woman interested in his money and fame. She should have realized it from the beginning, Lee supposed, but she would have refused to so much as fly out for a visit if she had. She lied to herself because she wanted to be with Roddy, and at the moment it almost wasn't worth the pain.

Almost. Even now, she had to admit that she had never been happier in her life than the months she spent with Roddy, even if it was all a sham. That there had also been many moments of loneliness and misery didn't matter. She had loved being with Roddy, but he ripped her heart out with his accusations. All this time, she had hoped her feelings were not one-sided, and that their relationship would develop some sort of permanence. Even now, knowing that was only an unrealistic fantasy wasn't enough to make her regret the time she spent with him.

But she couldn't go back. A girl had to have her pride.

Lee didn't just play their argument over and over in her head, she also gave a lot of thought to what had become of her over the past months. In hindsight, she saw she had made a number of mistakes in her relationship with Roddy, mistakes that likely contributed to his low opinion of her. She should not have given up everything that was hers in order to live in his shadow and play by his rules. She should have insisted on finding a job and renting her own place somewhere. She should have been more concerned with her future, and not just what she would wear to the next party or premiere. Lee had been putting her life on hold. It was more fun to live in the present and take everything day by day than to concern herself with things that hadn't happened yet.

The sun was up now, and her eyes felt gritty. Lee had spent the night in an uncomfortable plastic chair at the airport, reluctant to call any of her friends and tell them the story of how Roddy really felt about her. She also knew that Roddy would never think to look for her there. Being at the airport also made it easy to decide whether she should stay in California or return to Minneapolis.

When she still hurt just as much in the morning light as she had the night before, and she still felt reluctant to go back to Roddy and hear more ugly accusations, Lee decided to finally make use of the second half of her round-trip ticket. She only needed her driver's license to pick it up at the airline counter. With no baggage to declare, the only thing left to do was sit down again and wait for her flight to be called.

She spied the credit card in her wallet while arranging for her ticket, so as soon as that business was complete, she sat down and cut the card into tiny little pieces. She was all done shopping on Roddy O'Neill's dime.

That simple act filled her with resolve, so it was with a straight spine that Lee boarded a plane for Minneapolis. She had nothing but the clothes on her back and fifty dollars. She felt like tossing the money in the trash since it was technically *Roddy's* fifty dollars, but she was levelheaded enough to realize she needed a little cash until she got home. Everything else she gleefully left behind. She wanted nothing from Roddy, and nothing to remind her she had once been his.

Thank God she had held onto her apartment. She had thought about letting it go a couple of times, but at least had been smart enough not to do it. Now, she had her own place to stay while she recovered from her mortal wounds. The last thing she wanted right then was to be a burden on anyone else. Lee Miller would stand on her own two feet again.

During the flight, Lee thought about her father. She hadn't concerned herself with him in a long time. He so rarely called her for any reason, she tried to put him out of her mind. Now, she thought about him long and hard, just so she wouldn't think about Roddy. The last time she saw her father had been almost a year ago at Christmas when she stopped by his small Northeast Minneapolis house to exchange holiday greetings and drop off a gift. He had looked old and tired, but had been so offhand with her, she ignored it and left as quickly as she could.

She wondered what the old man would think of a visit from her now? Only someone living in a cave wouldn't know where she had been for the past several months. What would her father think of her taking off and leaving everything behind to live with a rock star? He would no doubt liken her to her mother, who had also left her responsibilities behind to run off with a man. On the other hand, maybe not. Maybe her father would be like almost everyone else and actually be impressed that Lee had attained some level of notoriety.

Of course, that was all in the past now. She was no longer Roddy O'Neill's girlfriend. She no longer lived in Beverly Hills and would be attending no more parties or premieres in leather and denim.

And it served no purpose to mope about it. She was better off getting out now, while she was still in one piece. Roddy didn't care about her. He liked the extra publicity she brought to the table, but the minute the media tired of the two of them, he would have dumped her and moved on to someone new.

Thinking about Roddy made her heart ache. She was still grappling with the fact that her dear, sweet Roddy had accused her of being cold-blooded and calculating. It was unbelievable that the same man who had made love to her with such single-minded intensity, as if nothing else in the world mattered, thought she even cared about money and fame. How could he think such things? How could she have been so wrong about him all this time? Why did she still want to go back?

"Miss? Fasten your seatbelt please. We'll be landing in a few minutes." A pretty stewardess shook her out of her reverie, and Lee did her best to give the woman a smile.

With no luggage, departing the airport was a breeze. Lee had quite frankly forgotten that the weather in Minnesota was much different from California in November, and the cold air hit her with an unpleasant blast when she stepped outside. She didn't care about the cold, though. It actually felt good to be just as cold on the outside as she was inside.

Now back on Minnesota soil, it was time to eradicate Roddy O'Neill from her mind. That was easier said than done, and Lee knew she would need a crutch. She was in no mood to be with friends who would console her. At the moment, she couldn't stand the thought of anyone trying to make her feel better. She wanted to wallow in her misery a little while longer, so that she never forgot how it felt.

Lee knew there was one person who would be perfect for just that sort of thing. Her father had never failed to bring each of her glaring faults to light. Why not drop in and pay him a visit?

With this thought in mind, Lee took the train to downtown Minneapolis, where she then transferred to a bus that would take her to her father's house. It was almost comforting to use something as familiar as Minneapolis mass transit.

Her father answered his door in a flannel shirt, baggy blue jeans, and his stocking feet. He seemed shocked to see her, whether for the mere fact of her presence or that she was supposed to be in California, she wasn't sure.

"Hi, Dad," she said airily as he let her in. Noting his odd look, she cast a glance at her wrinkled white shirt and heavily creased olive leather pants.

She had caught him doing what he always did. The TV was on, and an inane potato chip commercial blared through the uncomfortable silence while Lee stared defiantly at her father.

He just gazed quizzically at her.

"Well," she said finally, "aren't you going to welcome me home?"

"Did a few months out in California rob you of your good sense?" he snapped. "Where's your coat?"

His words lacked any venom, though, and Lee realized it was his way of trying to banter with her. The short sentences were his way of telling her he knew where she had been and what she had been up to. For some odd reason, probably because she was so destroyed on the inside, she found comfort in it.

She shrugged. "I just got in. I haven't stopped by my place yet."

"Come in and sit down. Want a beer?"

"Sure," she said quickly, sensing a slight change in her father's demeanor since the last time she had been to see him.

He padded off to the kitchen and returned with a couple cans of beer. He popped one open for Lee and handed it to her with a warm smile.

"Left him, huh?" he asked with amazing insight.

She simply stared in response, and he shrugged.

"I could tell. Nobody in their right mind wanders around Minnesota without a coat on this time of year."

"Yeah, I left him." The words sounded so cold and final, she actually winced.

"Not easy, huh?"

If Lee wasn't mistaken, it actually sounded as if her father cared. It was all the provocation she needed to pour her heart out to him.

"He accused me of using him for the attention and the money," she explained.

"How did you happen to meet a guy like him, anyway?" her father wanted to know.

She poured out the whole story about how she had been a big fan of Roddy's since she was a teenager, and how Debbie got them backstage passes for his concert. She left out the part about going back to Roddy's hotel room and making love for most of the night, though. She didn't think her father really wanted the details on that part of the story. Wistfully, she told him how Roddy had anonymously sent her flowers every week for two months before he finally appeared in the library.

"And you went back to California with him?" Her father seemed genuinely interested in her story.

"No. He got called back and I didn't hear from him for several more weeks. Then he called me one day and asked me to come out for a vacation. I wound up staying."

"And then yesterday, you realized you missed Minnesota and your old man, so you decided to come home, huh?" His tone was light, but her father's eyes were concerned.

Lee felt a pang of guilt for not telling her father about it before, but she honestly had not thought he would care. Now, she realized that he did care, but simply wasn't very good at showing it.

She smiled sheepishly. "Actually, it wasn't until Roddy accused me of using him for his money and a piece of the spotlight before I realized how much I missed Minnesota." She deliberately left out any reference to her feelings about her father. "Roddy apparently only needed me for publicity."

"He told you this?"

She took a long swig of beer before answering. "Not in so many words, but when he came home and found me playing the guitar..."

"When did you learn to play the guitar?"

"In California. I thought...well, it doesn't matter. Roddy got angry when he found out, and he accused me of using him until I could get my own band together, or something."

"I can't imagine you burst into tears and ran off."

Lee smiled a little at that. "No, I punched him before I walked out. And here I am." She meant to sound tough, but the effort failed when she dissolved into sobs.

"It's okay," her father said into her hair as his arms came around her. "If he's any kind of man at all, he didn't mean it. He'll come back for you."

She shook her head. "No, he won't. He told me we don't have a future." Well, at least he had said he couldn't promise her a future, and now she knew why. "He already came here for me once. It won't happen again."

ଔ

Lee's words were distressingly prophetic. Three weeks passed since she came home, and in all that time there had been not one word from Roddy.

He was apparently living it up now that she was out of the picture. She had seen several pictures of him in the gossip rags with women who looked like Eddie's castoffs. She may as well never have existed. Because she wasn't famous in her own right, there was no mention of her or their break-up whatsoever.

Unexpectedly, Lee spent a few days with her father, and they caught up on a lifetime of lost moments while she prepared herself to face the world again. It had seemed odd at first that she went to her father when she needed comfort, and she supposed that on a subconscious level she knew he really did care about her, and it was natural to go to the man who had raised her. Now, she was assailed by memories of the times her usually gruff father had offered comfort when she was hurt or lonely as a child. If nothing else, having Roddy break her heart had at least restored her relationship with her father.

Lee needed money, since fifty dollars didn't go very far in the modern world. She knew she would have to get a job as soon as possible, and wondered if Mr. Eggers would forgive her for running out on him.

He just happened to be out front helping a woman when Lee walked into the library. Eggers stopped talking mid-sentence when he saw her and almost rudely excused himself from his customer. He obviously couldn't believe his eyes, since Lee was supposed to be in California, lying by a pool or attending a glittery party. Instead, she walked defiantly into the library in jeans, high tops, and a denim jacket.

Lee knew she had changed during the months of her absence. She was no longer so ready with a smile, though the rest of her appeared to have thrived in the sunshine. Her long, wild hair was streaked, and her formerly white skin had a golden glow. If not the picture of happiness, she knew she at least looked healthy.

With a glance, she knew Eggers realized her relationship with Roddy was over. Why else would she be there, in Minnesota, in the library, when winter was just about to start? The knowledge was in his eyes when he approached.

"Lee," he said with a smile on approach. "I'm glad to see you're back."

She did her best to smile. "It's nice to see you, too, Mr. Eggers. How are things at the library?"

He shook his head and clucked his tongue. "Not the same at all since you left. Debbie is threatening to leave if I don't find a decent replacement for you soon. The last three people we tried were a nightmare."

In his own subtle way, he was telling her he wanted her back, and Lee suppressed the urge to hug him for it. She knew her emotions were out of control these days, which she supposed was natural when she lost the love of her life and regained her father all in the space of a few days. And now, someone whose reception she had been unsure of was welcoming her back.

Her smile was less forced now. "Funny you mention that," she said. "I came in here looking for a job."

He shrugged. "I might as well take you back. I won't have to train you."

"Thank you, Mr. Eggers." Her words were mild and she only squeezed his forearm instead of enveloping him in a bear hug, but she was sure he saw the relief in her eyes.

Debbie was shocked to see her, as Lee had not yet called any of her friends to let them know she was back in town. She was happy Lee was there, but sad that her fairytale life had ended and that Roddy was now in her past.

Lee's life became monotonous all over again, but it was a different kind of boredom than she had faced in Beverly Hills. There was no color in her life now, and nothing to liven up her nights, so she welcomed the repetition. She wasn't ready to get out in the world and live a real life filled with people again. Just having a place to go every day and set tasks to perform were enough.

Debbie invited Lee to get out and have fun, but Lee found that she now preferred to spend time with her father. It was better to solve the issues of her past than to deal with the issues of her present, and it really was balm for her soul to repair her one solid familial relationship.

She realized that the view was different from her father's perspective. Once they were able to talk about everything, she realized he had never blamed her for her mother's actions. He had simply loved her mother a great deal, and she broke his heart when she left. Lee looked a lot like her mother, and as time passed, her father began to avoid her, uncomfortable with the memories she evoked. Things had really only started to go south when she hit her teens, though, and her father had no idea how to react to her. His emotional distance made her resentful, which only compounded their issues, and over time their relationship all but died. By then, both of them had accepted they would never be close, but it had hurt him when Lee left without a word.

Lee's forgiveness was instantaneous, though she knew she would have behaved differently under the circumstances. If she had Roddy's baby, she would lavish all her love on the child once he was gone. Lee was wise enough to know that everyone reacted to grief in a different way, and acknowledged the part she had played in her relationship with her father. It was never too late, and they were becoming close now.

At the moment, her father was her rock. Without him there, she might have caved and called Roddy because she missed him so much. She missed hearing his Maserati pulling into the driveway every day, and missed the long, slow, burning looks she and Roddy shared when they were out in public. She missed the caresses they had shared when they were alone, and just being able to talk and laugh with him.

She wondered more than once whether she had made the right decision when she left. Sometimes she thought she should have stayed and tried to talk about the things he said to her. Roddy hadn't been himself that day, and he was under a lot of strain. She knew that didn't excuse his accusations, just because he had caught her playing the guitar. Besides, if he really meant those things, talking about it would have solved nothing.

The biggest clue of all was that he did not call. If he hadn't meant the things he said, he would certainly have contacted her by now. Lee also remembered he had never told her he loved her and never promised her a tomorrow. From all reports, he was happier being on his own again, and she would be better off just forgetting him.

CHAPTER SEVENTEEN

Roddy O'Neill didn't seem to have a care in the world. Eddie knew him, though, and knew Roddy's new lifestyle just wasn't natural. It might have been five years ago, but Eddie had been there when Roddy made the transition, and knew Roddy wasn't really interested in resuming his old ways. In the past few years, Roddy had become much more serious about his life and his music, and far more selective about his women. The moment Lee left, though, all bets were off.

The morning after their fight, Roddy had called and said, "She's not back."

"I'll find her," Eddie promised.

And so he had, but apparently too late. After trying everyone Lee had ever made an acquaintance with in LA, he checked the train and bus stations and the airport, and using his charm and influence, found out she had gone back to Minneapolis on the other half of her ticket. She was safely back in her dull little library again.

Roddy must have said something that cut deep, Eddie mused with a shake of his head. It had been obvious how much Lee loved his best friend, even if he was too stupid to see. She had to have been deeply hurt to leave everything behind the way she did. Eddie knew Roddy had earned his bad boy reputation, but he was different with Lee, and it was disappointing to everyone who knew Roddy that she was gone.

After she left, Roddy turned to music for solace. Eddie was afraid he would shut down and quit working again with Lee out of the picture, but he had done the exact opposite. He worked himself so hard, his mother even started to worry. He worked the band so hard they threatened mutiny.

There was one small group of people who benefited from Roddy's heartbreak, though. The record company executives reaped huge profits from his hard work and had even begun to insinuate that Roddy should start to plan another world tour. His new heartrending songs about lost love and emotional destruction were his best work yet. Coupled with his earlier songs about happiness and contentment, the disk would jerk listeners' hearts every which way and leave them wanting more. The record company smelled a hit, and was almost rubbing its hands together with glee.

It made Eddie feel sick. Such mercenary behavior was not rock and roll! It was just cold-blooded business. Roddy's label wanted to milk him for blood when he was at his lowest, and Eddie feared it might make Roddy collapse into some of his old, unhealthy habits if they weren't stopped.

Roddy was more than a little drunk when Eddie voiced his concerns.

"Change record labels?" he bellowed. "Are you crazy?"

"Are you blind? These guys are not the same ones who signed you," Eddie reasoned. "They harassed you when we weren't putting out music fast enough, and now they're trying to use your emotional state to sell records. It's not right."

Roddy's bleary stare was cynical. "We're making money, too."

Eddie then said something he never thought he would say. "Don't we have enough money? We're already rich. I want us to stay, and we're not going to last more than a couple more albums if this keeps up."

"Bull," Roddy countered obstinately. "I'm fine. I just feel like working hard right now."

"We can afford to slow down a little," Eddie argued. "Our last disk is still going strong. We're not some plastic top-forty band that relies on getting a new song out every six weeks so nobody forgets who they are. We're serious rock and rollers who already have a few classics out there from years ago. We don't need to have a new disk in stores in six months."

There was cold, hard steel in Roddy's eyes. "You seem to have forgotten whose band this really is."

Eddie just shut up so he wouldn't pop Roddy in the nose. He was obviously too drunk and messed up to know what he was saying. If he fired Eddie, it wouldn't be the first time. Eddie knew they would make up by the end of the week. He didn't have to worry about employment, in any event. He could have a new set-up by sunrise if he wanted, but he rather enjoyed playing with Roddy O'Neill. He and Roddy worked quite well together, and Roddy needed him, even if he was being too stubborn to realize it. The best thing would be to leave Roddy alone to ponder his words and then bring it up again later when he was sober.

That moment never came. Roddy was sober during the daytime while he worked his ass off on the new album, but the minute they wrapped for the day, he cracked open a bottle of something and made a beeline for the nearest party. There, he sat in a corner and let all the women his nasty attitude didn't repel hover around and get their picture taken with him.

Eddie followed Roddy around to keep an eye on things. That Roddy was going to crack soon seemed obvious. Eddie vowed to be there when it happened so he could get him back together. Naturally, this meant that both Roddy and Eddie now appeared at every hot party being thrown, and the trade magazines went crazy with wild stories of their imagined escapades. Anyone who heard the real story would probably have been bored stiff.

"PARTY DAYS ARE HERE AGAIN!" one headline proclaimed. Under it was a story about how Eddie and Roddy had grown tired of the quiet existence they had been living and now, both single once again, they were living it up in the thick of Hollywood night life. Their photos were snapped almost constantly. It had been ages since the two of them got wasted at parties together and no photographer wanted to miss his shot.

Eddie made use of the girls, and Roddy emptied the bottles. Once he got good and drunk, he always tired of the adoring women, insulted them until they had no choice but to leave him alone, and then staggered home in the early dawn hours.

ෆ

Roddy no longer enjoyed going home. It was there that he couldn't ignore the pain in his heart, or the way Lee's ghost had invaded every inch of the place. His house was huge and empty without her. Though he no longer wanted to be there, it seemed to be the only place where he could get away from both Eddie and the hordes of photographers at the same time.

His house was definitely haunted now. In the kitchen, he saw visions of Lee across the table, laughing with him while they ate. His game room assailed him with images of her bent over the pool table, attempting shots she could never make. His bedroom was strictly off-limits now. There was no way he could deal with the memories that lived there.

He wasn't safe outside, either. By the pool, he could hear Lee's laughter ringing across the water, see her lounging on one of the deck chairs, and almost feel her hot breath on his neck.

He felt like the worst kind of heel there was. Lee had loved him, and he wasn't so self-absorbed that it had come as a surprise when she threw the words in his face. It hadn't been enough to make him treat her right, though. It wasn't enough to make him follow his heart instead of his stupid ego. He had been arrogant enough to think he didn't have to offer her more than a roof over her head and a whirling social life because he was a rock star. Rock stars didn't have to make promises, or keep them if they hadn't signed anything. Why offer more to Lee when he was already giving her more than she had when they met?

By now, he hated himself for his selfish attitude. Lee was always honest, and he used it against her. She hadn't loved her job, or her home, and she didn't really have a family. What did she have to lose by coming to live in a nice, big mansion in Beverly Hills and being allowed to shop every day? In hindsight, he realized that a more established, secure woman with a strong father figure and some set goals would have demanded more from him. He had always known it, he supposed, and used it against her, and now he was the loser.

Lee wasn't coming back. If he crawled all the way to Minneapolis on his hands and knees and begged her forgiveness, it still could not erase all the things he said to her, and it wouldn't make up for all the times he had treated her like she was less than him. She would probably punch him again, just like he deserved, and slam the door in his face.

It was just like life to hand him the one woman who was right for him, and then take her away just as he was realizing how necessary she had become. He knew fate wasn't at fault, though. The blame was all his for ignoring his mother and everyone else who gave a damn about him and not listening when they told him he had to offer something more to Lee.

He wasn't so delusional he hadn't realized she wasn't completely happy, but rather than offering her a secure future, he had gone out to buy her another present. Now, he was stuck with a piece of real estate he didn't need, and the realization that it wasn't what Lee really wanted from him at all.

He ignored the way his heart screamed in agony as he trudged up the stairs and down the hall to the room he had been so happy to share with her. He hadn't crossed the threshold since the night he chased her away. Slowly, so as not to rouse any sleeping ghosts, he pushed the door open and went in.

The room was tidy, as Rosa was not afraid of Lee's ghost. The bed was made, the carpet bore signs of a recent vacuuming, and the mirrors boasted not a single speck of dust. Roddy left boot prints in the carpet as he made his way over to the closet and opened the door.

His eyes soaked in every detail when he turned on the light. His side of the closet was almost a dull monotony of black and faded blue, but Lee's side was a riot of color. Of its own volition, his hand reached out to touch her things. The leather jacket he touched felt soft enough to melt under his fingers. He spotted an outfit she had worn to a western premiere with him and smiled at the memory. Next, he recognized a purple suede dress she had worn to a party. He knew he would never forget the yellow dress of tight leather and fluttering feathers she had worn their first night out on the town together. There were so many outfits in such varied colors, it made his head spin. He frowned at the ice-blue sequined gown she had intended to wear to an awards show with him. It had gone unworn because the ceremony occurred after she left. But his undoing was her slightly beat-up acid-green biker jacket, the garment that had told him she was different from the first moment he laid eyes on her.

He remembered removing it from her the first time, tossing it negligently on the floor as he urgently went after her other clothes. He recalled the way she had hid her body from him in it while she hunted for her tee-shirt. He remembered it was the last thing he saw as the door closed behind her when it came time for him to leave. The jacket was such a vital part of his memories of Lee, he couldn't imagine her being without it.

Someday, Roddy knew, someone sane was going to come into his house and make him get rid of all of her things. He vowed the jacket was the one thing he wouldn't let them take away. He decided he would be buried with it.

He plucked the jacket off its hanger and brought it up to his face to inhale its scent. It smelled so much like Lee, he knew it would be a sacrilege if another woman even touched it. Feeling suddenly old, broken, and tired, he sank down to the floor beneath her row of brightly-colored clothes. Slow, hot tears splattered on the jacket as Roddy finally allowed himself to properly mourn her loss, and the pace at which he'd been driving himself collapsed him into sleep.

༄

Eddie gritted his teeth and shook his head when he found Roddy in the closet several hours later. It was obvious Roddy had finally cracked, and now

Eddie was angry with Lee. What could Roddy possibly have done to be reduced to *this*?

Impatient now, he shook Roddy awake. "Hey, Roddy! Don't you think you'd be more comfortable in bed?"

"I am in bed," Roddy mumbled without opening his eyes.

Eddie kept his voice calm when he said, "No, you're not. You're in your closet."

Roddy's red eyes flew open, and he was obviously upset he had been found in such a state. Eddie knew he would bear the brunt of it.

"What are you doing here?" he asked with a glare.

Eddie ignored the question and asked one of his own. "Why don't you just go get her back?"

Roddy slowly swung his gaze over to meet Eddie's. "Because she won't come back. I screwed up, Eddie, and she doesn't want to be here anymore. I've got nothing she wants."

Eddie was sure that wasn't true, but it was obvious Roddy believed it.

"I'm just going to work my way through this," Roddy went on, "and if I stay out of this closet and sleep in a different room until I sell this place, I'll be fine."

"Okay, great. What do you say we get out of the closet right now?" Eddie suggested. "It's kind of depressing in here."

As he grimly helped his best friend to his rather unsteady feet, Eddie had a somber thought. It was time to take matters into his own hands.

CHAPTER EIGHTEEN

Lee wiped her brow with the back of her hand. After lugging six huge reference volumes across the library from the Research & Cataloging Department, she was hot and sticky, and somewhat exhausted. She put the books in a pile while she caught her breath and then folded her feet delicately under herself as she sank down to the floor to shelve them. Her straight black skirt rode up on her thighs somewhat, but since there was no one around and she would be getting back up in a few seconds, she let it be.

She pulled one of the heavy books into her lap and shoved it onto the shelf with a grunt. Rubbing her shoulder, she reached for the next book. Something across the room caught her eye as she did so, but it couldn't possibly be what she thought, so she shook her head and got back to the task at hand. As she reached for the third volume, she saw it again, only this time it wasn't on the other side of the room.

Lee dropped the book and shifted her line of vision directly to a pair of beat-up snakeskin boots.

Roddy! her mind screamed. He had come back for her. He didn't mean the things he said and he was going to take her away again and…but wait. It wasn't Roddy.

Before she even got past the boots she knew it wasn't him. The stance was all wrong; arrogance without true confidence. Her eyes traveled slowly upward, over thighs bulging under worn denim, the expanse of chest covered by a lewd tee-shirt, and up to the handsome face and riot of dark hair.

"Eddie," she said, striving to keep the disappointment out of her voice.

He stood only a few feet away, and appeared to be staring at the exposed bits of thigh her bunched-up skirt had revealed. Lee almost rolled her eyes at his predictability, but at the same time it gave her a rush of familiar warmth. Eddie was a staple in the life she had left behind.

"That's what I've always liked about you, Lee," he drawled on a smile. "You're so good for my ego. I bet you give your landlord a more enthusiastic greeting when your rent is late."

She smiled at that, before her brows drew together. "What are you doing here, Eddie? Where's Roddy?"

Eddie looked at his boots while he answered. "He's in California." When Lee's face immediately fell, he added, "Killing himself."

"What?" Lee asked rather breathlessly. It hadn't occurred to her that Roddy might be in some kind of trouble.

"That's what happens when a guy works eighteen hours a day and parties for the other six because he can't stand to go home anymore," Eddie explained.

She shrugged and tried to ignore the little thrill she felt. "I've seen the pictures, Eddie. He seems to be having a rather good time."

Eddie smiled smugly and reached into his back pocket to pull out a small stack of photos. "I took these when he wasn't having such a good time," he said as he handed them over.

Lee gasped at the images. Roddy's eyes were red-rimmed and he looked like he was so tired he might drop. He appeared grim and lifeless.

She couldn't look Eddie in the eyes when she handed them back. "I had to leave, Eddie," she said unsteadily.

He shrugged. "Maybe you did. But now you have to come back. Roddy needs you."

Tired of looking up at him, Lee struggled to her feet. "Did he send you here to bring me back? Did he change his mind about the way things are?"

"No." Eddie's quick, loud denial had several heads turning to stare. "Nothing has changed, Lee. Roddy loved you, and he still loves you now."

Her laugh was derisive. "Ha! Roddy threw money at me, which didn't take much out of him, but that's all you have to do if you're a rock star, right?"

Her barb hit its mark and she saw him wince before he made an obvious effort at control.

"Obviously not," was his response. "Roddy doesn't have you anymore."

"Why are you here, Eddie?" Lee demanded with some impatience, suddenly tired of parrying with him.

"Because Roddy needs you," was his simple answer. "He's falling apart, and you and I both know it's because he doesn't care about himself or anything else without you."

"If he wants me back, why are *you* here?"

"Because he thinks you don't love him anymore."

"Maybe I don't."

Eddie sighed and ran a hand through his hair. "You don't even know how you changed him. You don't know how he was before he met you."

"And how was that?"

Eddie smiled. "Actually, he was kind of a dickhead. He pissed people off, said whatever he felt like, and told everybody if they didn't like it they could take a hike." At the look on her face, he chuckled. "I know he wasn't like that with you. And when you were around, he wasn't like that with anyone. I know he hurt you with some stupid stuff he said, but I also know he didn't mean it."

"You weren't there."

"No, but I was with him all day, and I know what kind of mood he was in. He had a seriously bad day, and I know that doesn't excuse the way he acted, but it's a reason. You were right to slug him, and maybe even right to take off. But you shouldn't have left town. If you had gone to his mom's or Helene's, Roddy would have been there the next morning, apologizing on his knees. But you were already gone, so he didn't get the chance."

Lee felt like burying herself in a stack of books. What Eddie said was true. She should have stuck around and tried to get to the bottom of things and work them out. Instead, she gathered all her insecurities around her like a cloak and fled.

Where did that leave her now? Part of her wanted to follow Eddie back to California and return to her life with Roddy. Maybe what Eddie said was true and he did love her and wanted her back. If it was true, she would hate herself forever if she didn't return. On the other hand, she knew she couldn't go back to the same life she had been living in Beverly Hills. She wanted Roddy back, but the circumstances could not be the same this time.

Lee met Eddie's eyes. "You're right, I didn't give him a chance to apologize and make it right," she said quietly. "But, Eddie, he made a point of not promising me a future. Maybe I shouldn't have run, but it seemed like the right thing to do since my days were already numbered."

"Maybe you should have demanded more from him," Eddie mused. "Maybe you should demand it now."

Lee just stared at him for a long moment, and then she gave him a small smile. "Why don't you give me a minute to talk to my boss, and then I want to take you to meet somebody."

She returned a few minutes later, after speaking with a rather resigned Mr. Eggers, and followed Eddie out to his car. It wasn't his Mercedes, but was a rather unassuming rental that brought a smile to her lips.

Eddie didn't ask where they were going, but followed her directions to the northeast side of town. They pulled up in front of her father's small house in its quiet neighborhood, and Lee led the way to the front door, where she knocked briskly.

Her father answered the door wearing a puzzled expression. Lee was expected to be at work for several more hours, and Eddie's presence confused him.

"Hi, Dad," Lee said as he let them in. "There's someone I want you to meet."

Realization dawned almost instantly, and her father smiled. "So, this is him. I told you he'd come back for you."

Lee's face fell. "Actually, no. Roddy is still in California. This is Eddie, a friend of his."

"Hi," Eddie said with a proffered hand.

Her father shook it and bluntly asked, "Where's Roddy?"

Before Eddie could reply, Lee cut in. "Roddy couldn't come, Dad. Eddie can explain it all to you."

With that, she left them standing in the living room and went into the kitchen.

଼

Thomas Miller stared at the long-haired young man in his living room while the guy in question casually perused the contents of his house. After a moment, Thomas offered his guest a seat.

Once settled, he turned and asked, "Would you mind telling me what's going on?"

Eddie shrugged and smiled. "At this point, I'm not really sure. I flew in today to talk to Lee. I asked her to come back to California."

"She just came back here because of that friend of yours," Thomas reminded him.

"I know that, but it was a mistake. She needs to come back home. Her life is in California now. She and Roddy had a fight, and he said some stuff, but he needs her."

"Maybe you should fill me in on a few details," Thomas suggested. The story was bound to be even more interesting told from this young man's perspective.

Eddie smiled and warmed to his tale. "Roddy lost the fight the first night he saw her. Something happened the second they met. I saw it with my own eyes. We had to go back on the road the next day, but he came back to visit her after the tour. Afterwards, he still couldn't forget her, so then he invited her out for a vacation."

"I already know all that."

"Well, you see, Mr. Miller," Eddie continued carefully, "Roddy isn't your average boy next door. I mean, a normal guy would have told her he loved her to distraction and couldn't live without her, right?" Thomas nodded, and he went on. "Words like that don't come easy to Roddy. Hell, *feelings* like that are new territory for him. So he fell back on what he knew and threw money at Lee. It was supposed to be enough."

"And it wasn't."

"No. Lee doesn't care about money. She was there because she loved him. So when Roddy picked a fight with her and accused her of being like other women, she high-tailed it out of there."

"And you're telling me this Roddy guy is miserable now without her."

Eddie nodded. "Yeah. I'm really worried about him. He's killing himself."

Thomas raised a brow. "What about all the articles in the magazines I see at the grocery store?"

Eddie raked a hand through his hair. "It's all a bunch of made-up BS."

"There have been pictures."

"That's all there have been. He hasn't, uh, taken anyone home or anything. He just gets obnoxious and wasted."

Despite himself, Thomas smiled. How well he remembered his own youth and its attendant dramas. He felt he had a pretty clear picture of Lee's life in California by now, and though he hadn't met this Roddy O'Neill character, it was obvious his daughter was in love with him. The guy had a friend who was good enough to intervene when the lovers were too stubborn to solve their own problems, too, which spoke well of his character. He supposed he could step up and lend a hand, as well.

"I hope your friend doesn't think everything is just going to go back to the way it was," he said gruffly to Eddie.

"Huh?" The rocker looked confused.

"I mean, Lee isn't going back without a real commitment."

"I can't speak for Roddy," Eddie hedged, "but he's a pretty smart guy. And I think at this point he's willing to do whatever she wants as long as she comes back."

"Let me talk to her for a minute," Thomas suggested, rising from his chair.

He left Eddie in his living room and found Lee at the kitchen table.

"Already making good use of your old man, huh?" he said as he came in.

Lee smiled radiantly. "I didn't know what to do, so I came to you. I want to go back, but I don't, you know?"

"I do. And I'm glad you came to me. I haven't always been a good father, and I'm glad you're giving me a chance to make it up to you."

"Thanks, Dad." Her eyes were shiny.

Silence hung in the air for several seconds before Thomas spoke again. "You need to go back," he told her. "You're in love with him and it's where you want to be. I didn't get a second chance with your mother, and I don't want you to throw yours away."

Thomas had never brought up Lee's mother before, so she looked at him in surprise.

"If I'd been different, she might not have left me," he continued. "But that's all water under the bridge. It's not too late for you and your rock star."

Lee got out of her chair and came around the table to hug her father. As he held her, he thought of all the time they had wasted and all the things they should have said over the years. Lee had been through enough in her young life, and it was time she got to experience some happiness. It wasn't over for him, either, and he was going to get some, too.

"I love you, Dad," Lee cried into his shoulder.

"I love you, too," he murmured as he stroked her hair. Then he straightened and gave her a little push. "Now, go get some bags packed and get yourself back to California with that greasy punk you brought into my house."

Lee smiled in pure happiness. "I think you should pack a bag, too, Dad," she suggested. "I want you to come with me. You need a vacation."

Now he was uncertain. "I don't know, Lee. I'm not all that fond of California."

"I want you to meet Roddy, Dad."

Thomas's heart melted instantly. After she left town for several months without a word to him, now his daughter finally wanted him to be a real part of her life. How could he argue with that?

CHAPTER NINETEEN

Lee walked out to the patio with her heart in her throat. She was nervous about seeing Roddy, afraid he didn't really want her back after all the weeks that had passed. Still, she took her courage in hand and went to see him anyhow.

She was glad she had come alone when she got her first glimpse of Roddy. She would not have wanted anyone else to see him sleeping in a deck chair with a foot carelessly thrown over each side. His hair was a mess, with no bandanna in sight. He was shirtless, and his shorts were filthy. His cheeks and chin also sported several days' growth of beard that Lee instantly decided did not suit him. There was a mess of empty cans and a cooler with its top tipped half off lying nearby. Lee almost couldn't believe the sorry state of affairs.

As Roddy snored, she seated herself a few feet away in the deck chair nearest his and simply stared for a long time.

"Roddy," she said finally, just loud enough to make his eyes flutter.

"I'm not hungry," he murmured sleepily.

"Open your eyes," Lee said firmly, only to regret it

when he did. They were an almost glowing red.

He blinked a couple of times in confusion. "Lee?"

"Yes," was all she said.

"Come here," he bade. "You're too far away."

She got to her feet and came to stand by his chaise. When she stopped, he reached out a hand and ran it over her leg.

Now satisfied she was real, he smiled. "You came home."

She dropped down to her haunches to look into his eyes. "Yes. If you still want me, I'm home."

His eyes clouded. "If I want you? Of course I want you. My life has been hell without you."

Their arms came around each other of their own accord.

"Mine too," Lee said against his chest.

"I missed you so much," Roddy said into her hair. "I'm never letting you go again."

Lee felt like she had died and gone to heaven. Roddy had not rejected her. Instead, the very first thing he did was give her the reassurance she had needed for so long. Being in his arms was the only place she wanted to be, and at the moment she wasn't sure how she had been able to leave.

After a moment, Lee drew back to look into his eyes. "I love you, Roddy," she said, done keeping her feelings to herself. "I'm sorry I left."

"I'm just glad you came back," he told her as he pulled her onto his lap. "And I should have told you a long time ago that I love you, too."

Lee felt a surge of absolute happiness and her arms tightened around him enough to cut off his circulation. She had hoped they could patch things up, but had not dreamed Roddy would proclaim his love for her the minute she got there. In fact, she had feared she would never hear the words at all.

"You do?" she heard herself ask in some disbelief.

He seemed startled she would doubt him. "Of course I do. I was an idiot for not saying it before. I was just an arrogant fool with you, Lee, and I hope you'll forgive me."

"I should have been more open with you about my feelings," she said, "but I was afraid."

"Me too."

"No way."

"Oh, yeah." Roddy chuckled. "You were never impressed by me, and I'm not used to that. I liked it, but I didn't quite know how to handle it."

"I'm glad I'm back," Lee said against his lips, "but in a way I'm also glad I went home."

Roddy stiffened, and she smiled gently.

"Do you remember the stuff I told you about my relationship with my father?" she asked.

"Yes."

"Well, when I went home, I felt so horrible, I decided I might as well pay him a visit. Roddy, he missed me while I was gone. We started talking when I got back, and now we have things pretty much straight between us, and we have a relationship."

Roddy hugged her. "That's wonderful. I always felt bad about that situation."

"My father came back to California with me," she added quickly.

"He what?"

"I wanted him to meet you."

Now Roddy looked scared. He apparently wasn't used to dealing with father figures. It wasn't likely the women who visited his dressing room introduced him to their parents, and this was new territory.

"I hope you warned him I'm not the boy next door," Roddy groaned.

"Roddy, my father lives in Minneapolis, not a cave," Lee said on a laugh. "He'll love you and I know you'll feel the same about him."

"Sure," Roddy agreed, but she could see he had a few reservations.

"He's hanging out with Eddie right now," Lee went on.

"Eddie? What's he doing with Eddie?"

Lee gaped at him in some surprise. "I'm here because Eddie came to Minneapolis to get me, Roddy. You didn't know?"

Roddy burst out laughing. "No, I had no idea. That son of a bitch; meddling in my life. Probably figured he owed me one after I got rid of Claire for him. I can't believe it."

"He shocked me half to death when he came to the library. For a second, I thought it was you. I almost died of disappointment when I realized it wasn't."

Roddy laughed again. "Eddie's going to need therapy to get over the inferiority complex you're giving him."

Lee laughed along with him. "I doubt that. He's far too sure of himself."

"But he is a good guy."

"He is," Lee agreed. "He wouldn't take no for an answer."

Roddy nuzzled her neck. "I'm forever in his debt," he murmured. "I'm so glad you came home. And I'm sorry I said what I did. It's not true, and I didn't mean any of it. You just freaked me out when I found you playing the guitar. It was kind of a shock, but I think it's really cool. And if you want to get into the music business, I'll help you any way you want."

"Seriously?"

Roddy nodded. "I had such a bad day that day. Everything went wrong, and then they brought out this dancer who looked just like you, only sleazier. All I could think about was getting the hell out of there and getting home to you. And then I got here and saw you playing the guitar, and I thought, aw hell, she wants to be in the business, too. I could see you dressed like that dancer, acting like all the other fake backstabbers I know, and I just lost it. I'm sorry I did. Even if you get into the business, you're still going to be you, and that will never change. I sure didn't mean to keep you trapped up here with nothing going on in your life."

Lee kissed him soundly. "I thought I knew you better than that, and it's a relief to know I was right. For the record, though, I do not want to be in the music business. I just learned the guitar so I could jam with you sometimes. I thought it would be fun, and I needed more to do. It never occurred to me to start a career with it, and your reaction really shocked me."

"I didn't mean it, Lee. I never wanted you to put your life on hold, and I did realize you were bored. In fact, I had just bought you a present I was hoping would help before you left."

"Oh? What was it?"

Roddy shook his head and smiled. "It's a surprise. I'll show you later. For now, I have something else for you."

"Oh really?" Lee raised a brow, knowing from the tone of his voice what he had in mind.

In answer, Roddy pulled her tee-shirt over her head and simply drank in the sight of her exposed flesh. His hands passed over her skin with the same care as an archaeologist with a priceless artifact. His hot lips followed, leaving a trail of fire wherever they went.

They tore the rest of each other's clothes off, feasting first their eyes, and then their hungry mouths, on each other. As if there had been no long weeks of separation, each remembered the things that most pleased the other. They got lost in the whirlwind of passion that left them breathless some time later.

Roddy turned to Lee afterwards and placed a kiss on her temple while she dozed. "Ready for your surprise?"

Her eyes came open and her brows furrowed. "Do me a favor first?"

"Name it."

"Shave off that stubble on your face. I hate it."

"Oh, really?"

He rubbed his jaw against hers, and when she squealed, he scraped his stubble against her neck and over a few other choice parts of her body. Lee leapt off the chaise, and he chased her up the stairs to their bedroom, which looked the same as it always had. Lee watched Roddy shave in the bathroom mirror, and then allowed him to back her into the shower, so it was quite some time before either of them remembered his surprise.

Roddy laced himself into a pair of tight white leather pants and threw an unbuttoned shirt on with them, then carefully tied a bandanna over his hair. As she watched him dress, Lee realized how much she had missed him while she was gone.

As she stood in the doorway to their closet, it struck her how much she had also missed her clothes. The person she was in Minneapolis didn't get to wear colored leather and miniskirts, and she understood just then how much of herself she had left behind.

Roddy's arms came around her and he broke into her reverie. "This is the first time I've really been in here since you left," he told her. "I visited once, but I never came back in after that. I've been sleeping down the hall."

"Oh, Roddy." Lee leaned against him and simply enjoyed the feel of his arms around her.

He let her go a moment later and told her to hurry up and get dressed in something sexy. Even though they weren't going out on the town, Lee happily delved into her collection and emerged with a snakeskin mini-dress and matching ankle boots that she knew Roddy loved. He always called it her special librarian outfit, which made them both laugh.

Lee pestered him for hints to the surprise, but

Roddy wouldn't give in. Instead, he bundled her into his Maserati and raced off into the gathering darkness. The car finally squealed to a stop in front of a garishly-lit, rundown bookstore on Sunset Boulevard.

"Here we are!" Roddy announced.

Lee looked around uncertainly. "Okay. Where's my present?"

"It's right here."

"Where?" Lee was still puzzled.

Roddy pointed at the bookstore. "There."

"The bookstore?"

"Yes. That's your present. On one condition."

Incredulous, Lee's mouth worked for several seconds before she finally said, "You bought me a *bookstore?* Only you, Roddy."

He shrugged. "You were bored, and I know you like books. I couldn't buy you a library, but I figured this was the next best thing. I know the place needs work, but I did that on purpose so you could fix it up however you like."

"When did you do this?"

"I bought it a few days before you left. I was just going to give it to you with no strings attached, but I changed my mind about that now."

She arched a delicate brow. "Oh?"

"I, uh, thought it would make a nice wedding present instead," he said, staring right at her.

"A wedding...oh." Lee was quite frankly stunned.

Roddy hastily took her hands in his and decided to do things the right way. "I love you, Lee, and I don't want to lose you ever again. I thought about a lot of things when you were gone. I know I want you in my life forever, and that means marriage. So…will you marry me?"

Lee was overcome with joy, and she flung herself across the car and into his arms, screaming, "Hell yes!"

If she wasn't mistaken, she saw tears in Roddy's eyes as he pulled her close and kissed her.

☙

Thomas Miller was just as nervous as Roddy about their upcoming meeting. He had dressed in a pair of pressed trousers and a carefully ironed shirt without a tie for the occasion. He wasn't a businessman and would not have been comfortable in a suit, but for some reason, he wanted to look respectable and somewhat authoritative when he met his daughter's lover.

Lee clung to Roddy's arm when they opened the door. She had a look of such rapt happiness on her face, Thomas vowed to like Roddy O'Neill no matter what.

A father could hope to have a more respectable-looking son-in-law, he supposed. Roddy's dirty-blond hair was as long as Lee's and he kept it under a wide bandanna. Thomas had never seen tighter pants on a man, though he supposed they cost more than a custom-made suit. The young man wore a tee-shirt that exposed what Thomas had been half afraid he would see: his daughter's lover had a collection of tattoos. Roddy didn't appear to be the knight in shining armor he had always pictured for his little girl, but Thomas knew the man was very successful, and he lived in a beautiful Spanish-style mansion that was obviously worth millions.

Thomas had seen Roddy O'Neill on TV before, though the reality of him was a bit more jarring than what he expected. Still, the shock of Roddy was nothing compared to seeing what the man had done to his daughter.

Other than the happily glowing look on Lee's face, Thomas hardly recognized her. She was stuffed into a pair of skin-tight velvet jeans in an unnatural green with a mostly-unbuttoned silk shirt in a rather iridescent shade of teal. She wore stiletto boots on her feet. The outfit was obviously expensive, but Lee's grandparents would turn over in their graves if they could see her in it.

"Hi, Dad!" she greeted him with enthusiasm. Thomas noted Roddy hung back with a look of trepidation on his face.

Lee stepped up and planted a big kiss on Thomas's cheek, smiling from ear to ear. He decided to be his most polite, just for her. There was such a contrast between the way she had been when she showed up on his doorstep a few weeks ago and the way she looked now, he vowed to do anything he could to keep her happy.

"This is Roddy," she introduced her boyfriend, who finally took a step forward and extended a hearty hand. "Roddy, this is my dad."

"Nice to meet you, Mr. Miller," Roddy murmured politely in a gravelly voice that evoked late nights, booze, and cigarettes.

"Hello, Roddy," Thomas greeted evenly. "Nice house you've got here."

"Thank you. Lee and I like it."

"Come out to the pool, Dad," Lee invited as she took his hand. "Rosa made some lunch."

From her demeanor, Thomas guessed Lee was up to something, and was probably enjoying making use of her dad. He decided he enjoyed stepping up for her. It bothered him that she had thought he didn't care about her for so much of her life, and he was determined to take the steps to right that wrong.

Lee led the way through an impressive house, past marble floors and expensive art to the patio. An aquamarine swimming pool glittered in the bright sunlight at the center, along with several chaises and an umbrella table situated in the shade. The patio sat above an inviting expanse of green lawn that stretched down to an adobe wall and a riot of flowering plants.

"Why are there only two places at the table?" Thomas wondered when he noticed the discrepancy.

Lee let go of his hand and smiled like a vixen. "Because you and Roddy are dining alone. Roddy has some things he wants to talk to you about, and I'm going out to reacquaint myself with some friends."

With that, she disappeared, leaving the two men who loved her to stare warily at each other.

"Have a seat," Roddy invited, still looking blatantly nervous.

Thomas sat at the brightly-set table with Roddy and gave him a fatherly look. "She knows how to wrap a man around her little finger when she wants, doesn't she?"

Roddy chuckled. "She does. The press here loves

her."

"And you?" Thomas surprised himself with the blunt question.

Roddy surprised him by looking dreamy. "Oh, yeah," the younger man said on a sigh. "She changed my life." He paused for a second and then looked directly into Thomas's eyes. "I want to marry her."

Thomas took a moment to digest that. Naturally, he had hoped that the man his daughter loved more than anything else on earth wanted to marry her, but he hadn't been quite prepared for the reality of Roddy. The man just didn't instill feelings of paternal security. Thomas knew it was just his looks, though. Lee had picked him, and his daughter had always had good sense.

"I see," he said finally when it was obvious Roddy expected him to say something. "I know you'll be able to take care of her, but you've got a reputation."

Roddy seemed stunned by his remark. He obviously hadn't expected to be grilled by Lee's father. Thomas was not a snob who looked down his nose at others, but Roddy had to know he also wasn't a pushover.

"I would never cheat on Lee," he promised fervently. "For one thing, she'd rip my heart out with her bare hands and stomp on it, and for another, I just couldn't do that to her."

"What about on concert tours? I've heard about what goes on during those."

Roddy smiled a little. "That's actually kind of how I met Lee."

Thomas scowled and Roddy chucked nervously.

No father wanted to hear the story of how his daughter had indulged in a night of debauchery with a rock star. Thomas had already figured out Roddy and Lee hadn't been playing cards that night, but he also didn't really want to hear about what actually happened.

"All that is in the past now," Roddy was quick to say. "I'll be taking Lee along with me on tour when I go again."

Thomas stared holes into him. "You better be sure this is what you want. I don't want Lee getting her heart broken later because you changed your mind."

"I'm almost thirty years old," Roddy said with his back up. "I think the wild part of my youth is behind me. Lee is what I want now."

Thomas's eyes made a slow perusal of Roddy's appearance once again, and he finally grunted and said, "I hope so."

He had to admit he wasn't exactly comfortable with the ruffian who had stolen his daughter's heart. Yet, after sharing lunch with the unusual young man, he realized Roddy was an intelligent, serious guy who knew what he wanted out of life and how to get it. His rebel appearance was part of his success, and Thomas would simply have to get used to it.

Thomas was thrilled when Lee told him Roddy had bought her a bookstore as a wedding gift. Not many men could afford to give their brides such a present, and it was certainly better than a pair of diamond earrings. Lee would no longer feel bored and useless with her own business to run.

Thomas and Roddy were amicably discussing work issues when Lee returned. Thomas was in the middle of giving Roddy his opinion on his record label, and Roddy was intently listening, when she appeared in the doorway to the house.

"Roddy told me the news," Thomas said when he saw her.

"And?" Her tone was expectant.

"I think I'm going to like my new son-in-law after all."

CHAPTER TWENTY

The California sun beat relentlessly down onto the greenery in Roddy's back yard. The smell of flowers was heady in the air. Not a single cloud marred the unending blue of the sky as sunlight glistened off the pool. Gardenias floated in the still water while the soft sounds of a string quartet warming up wafted on the air. Tables groaned under the weight of the huge trays of food displayed over every inch of space. A huge, white cake sat sentinel in the middle of it all, with a hand-painted bride and groom standing on the top layer, waiting for the festivities to begin.

Belying the peace of the scene were the dozens of red-jacketed waiters and waitresses who scurried about, laying on the final touches. They weaved around each other with their trays of food and skirted men in coveralls carrying stacks of folding chairs. The chairs were being set up in neat rows on the expanse of green on the lower part of the lawn while technicians set up lights and sound equipment.

Huge pots of flowers dotted the premises, their colors and scents mingling with the plants that grew on the grounds, and the whole setting looked like a fairytale land.

Margaret O'Neill surveyed her handiwork with a satisfied smile. It hadn't been easy to achieve, but her persistence had served her well, at least on the grounds. She was still a little worried about the goings-on in the house.

She turned on her heel with a slight frown. Roddy was creating problems. She had known he wasn't a conformist since he came home with a tattoo at the age of fifteen, but she had expected a little more cooperation from him on his wedding day. He had insisted he be allowed to wear a bandanna for the ceremony, and much to Margaret's chagrin, Lee sided with him on the issue. Only Margaret's persistence, along with Thomas Miller's, and their unexpected ally Eddie, had made them change their minds.

Margaret made her way back into the house to check in on her son one more time. She would have to keep a close eye on him that day if she wanted to keep him in line, and Margaret wasn't about to let him get away with anything during the wedding she had waited her whole life to arrange.

"This is my last chance to boss you around," she said in the face of his protests. "From now on, you'll have a wife to harass you, so let me enjoy this."

Lee was almost sweet enough to make up for Roddy's tantrums. From the first, she had relied heavily on Margaret's assistance. Margaret knew Lee's mother was nowhere around, and she gleefully accepted Lee as her daughter. She went with Lee to help her pick out her dress, and Margaret was the one who had insisted one should be created especially for her. When Lee balked at the cost, Margaret simply told her it was an excellent use of Roddy's money.

"This is probably my last chance to see you in a decent dress," Margaret had cajoled. "You're always in some tiny scrap of leather, and I want some pictures of you and Roddy looking respectable."

Lee never could resist Margaret when she acted motherly, and wound up finally agreeing to the pearl-encrusted, trailing white silk creation Margaret insisted on. She looked absolutely breathtaking in the dress, and Roddy probably wouldn't even recognize her.

Then again, Lee might not recognize Roddy, Margaret mused. Roddy's hair was pulled back neatly and he almost looked respectable. He was actually wearing shoes, rather than the cowboy boots he usually liked to clomp around in. His black silk tuxedo fit him to perfection, having been tailor-made to fit every hollow and bulge. If Lee was the slightest bit normal, she would insist Roddy dress that way more often.

Margaret let loose a happy sigh when she opened Roddy's bedroom door.

He turned to look at her, and his displeased scowl vanished. Marrying Lee was what he wanted, but the wedding plans were all Margaret's. She knew he and Lee went along with her plans to please her, and appreciated both of them for their cooperation.

"My son," she said on a smile. "You almost look respectable. I can't see any tattoos, and there's no hair in your eyes."

"Take a good look, Ma," he told her with a grin. "This is the first and last time you'll ever see me this way."

His smile turned to a scowl when Eddie approached with a bow tie.

Eddie was obviously having a good time. Roddy's groomsmen were all dressed in white tuxedos with red ties and cummerbunds. Margaret could tell Eddie liked the way he looked. His hair had been allowed to tumble free, unlike Roddy's, but Eddie pulled off the look with aplomb.

Guests began to arrive, and Margaret left her son in order to greet them and start the festivities. There would be no outside photographers during the ceremony, though there was one hired especially for the event, and Thomas had also hired a videographer. Afterwards, a few select paparazzi would be allowed in for a single hour to snap pictures to their hearts' content, which was a photographer's dream with Roddy's guest list.

ෆ

Down the hall in a guest room, Lee put the finishing touches on her appearance. Debbie was there to help her, along with Helene and two of her other California friends. Debbie and Helene got on famously, and Helene was already doing her best to convince Debbie she should relocate to the west coast and hook up with a musician. Lee smiled, stealing glances at them in the mirror as she touched up her makeup and let the hair stylist do amazing things to her usually unruly hair.

While Lee was dressed in blinding white, her bridesmaids all wore beautiful, deep red satin gowns. The color became her friends well, she decided. She smiled watching Debbie with her other friends, and chuckled as she remembered Mr. Eggers's dire warnings that he expected Debbie to return. Lee would let her go for now, she decided, but she was already thinking about luring Debbie back when she was ready to open her bookstore.

It was still hard to believe she was now a business owner. She and Roddy had talked, and they decided she should take a few classes to learn the things she needed to know to run the place. She was already looking forward to every aspect of the new venture.

She was most excited about renovating the store. The current stock ran toward fanzines and pornography, so she had decided to get rid of all the inventory and start over. Plans were already in place to gut the store and rebuild it shelf by shelf. Lee and Roddy excitedly discussed their plans every night, in between their feverish efforts to become reacquainted. Roddy was just as enthusiastic about every bit of it as she was, and was trying to talk her into opening a music section so he would have an excuse to hang out there.

Lee had never dreamed it was possible to be this happy. She had friends, in the plural. She finally had a loving father, and was gaining an excellent substitute for a mother. But most of all, she was going to start a real life with the man she loved.

Roddy could dissolve her with a glance. He could start her on fire with his touch. And when he made love to her, which was often, the entire earth shook with their passion.

Lee loved Roddy more than anything else in the

world, and knew that he loved her just as much. Without his money and fame, and the fine house in Beverly Hills, their feelings for each other would still be the same, she knew, but she was really grateful for all of it.

A loud knock at the door startled her out of her reverie.

"Lee!" her father called. "Are you girls ready? The preacher's here and we're ready to start the ceremony."

☙

A hush came over the crowd on the lawn as Lee wafted down the stairs on her father's arm. Lee didn't notice. She was too busy staring at the man who was shortly to become her husband.

Roddy looked different in a tuxedo with his hair pulled back. He was handsome that way, but she decided she liked him better in tight leather pants with a bandanna wrapped around his head. The red flower in his lapel looked out of place, and she vowed to remove it as soon as possible.

His eyes locked with hers as she floated down the steps. She smiled as she read the look in them. They were surrounded by well-dressed famous people on one of the most important days of their lives, but when they looked at each other that way, it was just the two of them. She knew he longed to rip her expensive silk dress off her and get her down to her skin. Despite the beauty of her gown and intricate hairstyle, she knew he preferred her in painted-on jeans and a tee-shirt with her hair loose and free. There were only a few more hours of formality to get through, though, and then they could be themselves again.

Roddy held her hand tightly in his as the preacher performed the short ceremony that brought them together. Afterwards, Roddy ravaged her mouth in a possessive kiss, and then led her up to the patio for the cake-cutting ceremony and the hour of popping flashes he was allowing the paparazzi.

Lee picked up the knife in an unsteady hand, but felt calmer when Roddy covered it with his.

He bent to kiss her cheek and murmured in her ear. "You're so beautiful, Lee. I hope all our kids look just like you."

"Kids?" Her heart fluttered suddenly.

His free arm wrapped around her waist and pulled her close. "I told you I'd keep you busy from now on."

The picture that was snapped in that moment was priceless.

The End

Made in the USA
Lexington, KY
02 July 2016